Unassuming Queen

Valentino Empire, Book 2

Kylie Kent

Ebook ISBN 13: 780645257250
Paperback ISBN: 978-1-922816-02-3

Cover illustration by
Stacy Garcia - Graphics By Stacy

Editing services provided by
Kat Pagan – https://www.facebook.com/PaganProofreading

This book contains scenes of sexual acts, profanity, and violence. If any of these are triggers for you, you should consider skipping this read.

To Reilly, my very own unassuming queen. You are literally the best thing since sliced bread.

Thank you for always making me laugh, for always being willing to talk plots with me, and for giving me endless content and ideas I will never consider using. But most of all, thank you for being the best friend a girl could ask for.

Chapter One

Holly

"Ti voglio bene. Tornerò appena posso. Don't forget, Holly." I wake with a jolt as T's voice whispers in my ear.

"T?" I question into the darkness, getting no response. It's been the same routine for the past three nights. I'm wearing one of his shirts, I have one of his suit jackets wrapped around me like a blanket, and I'm sleeping on the chair. Because I can't for the life of me get into the bed, knowing he won't be joining me. "When?" I yell into the emptiness. "When the hell are you coming back?" I pick up the glass of wine I left on the table next to me and throw it against the wall.

I've never endured a pain like this. I thought I knew grief after my brother died, but this is so much worse. It's like a part of me is dead too. *I feel dead.* I don't want to live a life where T doesn't exist. How can this happen? We've only had weeks together. This is not how our story was meant to end. How can someone you've known for such a short period of time seep so far into your soul that you're left with nothing but shattered pieces of who you were before them? How am I meant to go on, pretending I'm okay?

I'm not okay. This is not okay.

I need T. He has to come back. He just has to. Or I have to get to him. I know the thoughts running through my head right now are not good, but I can't live with this pain. And I can't live without *him.*

I pick up a piece of glass from the floor. Falling to my knees, I hold the broken shard to my face, staring at the ghost of my reflection. One slice. It would only take one *good* slice, and I'd be able to see him again.

The door opens in a frenzy, the heavy panel slamming against the wall. "Fuck! Holly, no. Put that fucking down. *Now.*" Neo rushes over to me, snatching the glass from my fingers. "This is not the fucking answer."

"I-I-I can't breathe." I heave as the tears fall down my face. I don't even care that he's seeing me cry. I don't care about anything anymore. I just need T.

"Shh, it's going to be okay. I've got you." Neo picks me up and carries me out of the bedroom. Sitting me on the sofa in the common area, he looks down at me for a moment before lifting me in his arms again, walking into the kitchen, and placing me on the stool at the bench. I let him move me around. What's it matter? It doesn't. Nothing does. "I'll make you some tea."

"Why is this happening? This wasn't meant to happen. I need him, Neo. I need him so much."

"I know, Hol, so do I," he says as he goes about boiling the kettle. He mumbles something under his breath in Italian, but I don't catch what he says.

"*Ti voglio bene. Tornerò appena posso*—what does it mean?" I ask.

Neo's body freezes, before he takes a deep breath and turns around. "Why?"

"I keep hearing it in my sleep. It's stupid, I know. But that's what Theo says in my dream. He said it to me on the phone that day too. I want to know what it means."

"He said that to you? Fucking idiot." Neo shakes his head. "You're far too smart for him, Holly."

"Don't say that about him. What does it mean?"

"It means: *I love you. I'll be back as soon as I can.*"

I repeat the words over and over in my head. *I'll be back as soon as I can.* Does that mean he's not really gone? I've had this niggling thought—this feeling in my gut—that he wasn't in that building when it blew up. But if he wasn't, where the hell is he? And why the bloody hell would he put me through all this pain?

"Here, drink this." Neo places a steaming cup in front of me. I don't take it. I don't want to drink it. I watch as Neo turns his back to me, pulling out his phone and texting someone. He gets an instant reply and curses in Italian; *those* are the words I've picked up on quickly.

I know it's probably my own wishful thinking, but I can't help but think he's texting T. Does he know where he is? What are they up to? The hope that blooms in my chest gives me something. And I need that *something*—to hold on to it—because it's this tiny flicker of optimism that will push me forward each day.

I'll be back as soon as I can. He's coming back. He has to. "Is he coming back?" I ask the question aloud this time, and Neo pivots to face me.

"No, Hol, he's not. I'm sorry it's not the answer you want to hear. But he's gone."

"I don't believe you. You're hiding something. Wait... did you do this? Did you arrange for him to be in that building when it blew up? You're his underboss, right? Which means you have a lot to gain with T gone." I stand and back away.

"What the fuck? No! You think you're the only one

hurting here? Guess what, princess? *You're fucking not.* Do you really think I wanna do this? To be stuck babysitting your ass while someone out there is responsible for killing my best fucking friend? No, I fucking don't. I shouldn't be here. I should be hunting down the fucker who took him from us."

"Then why aren't you?"

"Because of you, Holly. If anything happens to you, T will never fucking forgive me, dead or otherwise."

"What could possibly happen to me? You need to go and find who did this. I want their bloody head on a spike. I want to see them suffer. I want... I want T back!" I yell.

"We both do. So, tell me, Holly, just what were you planning to do with that piece of glass?" I don't look at him. I can't admit that the brief thought of ending it all, ending the pain, crossed my mind. "That's what I thought. You hurting yourself won't fix anything, Hol. Promise me you won't do something that fucking stupid." Neo stops in front of me, tugging me into an embrace.

It's not right. These aren't the arms I need wrapped around me right now. I pull away when there's a knock at the door. "Are you expecting someone?" I ask.

Neo puts his fingers to his lips, urging me to be quiet. Then he shakes his head, draws a gun, and walks to the door, ushering me along behind him. He glances at his phone before his body relaxes, and he tucks his weapon back into his waistband.

I can't see who's there, but I watch as he opens the door and scans up and down the hallway. "Really? Was that necessary?" Neo grunts as he looks to the ground.

"They weren't gonna let us in?" a rough voice replies—a voice I know very well.

"Bray?" I push Neo aside and am instantly pulled into my sister's arms. "Rye?" I question. How...? Why are they here?

I thought I already cried as much as I could, but the moment Reilly's arms are around me, I sob. I sob so hard I can't stay upright. She's holding me tight but struggles to bear my weight. "Bray, help," she says, and the next thing I know, Bray's carrying me back over to the sofa. "What happened? What the hell? You didn't fucking tell me she was this bad!" Reilly yells.

"I told you she needed you. I sent a fucking jet to get you here," Neo counters. "Bray, I need a word." He nods his head towards the kitchen.

"I don't know who the fuck you think you are, asshole. But if you ever speak to my wife like that again, there won't be any body parts for your loved ones to find," Bray growls.

Oh shit, my brother-in-law is hot-headed when it comes to my sister. They don't know about T's family. He doesn't know who he's threatening. He may be able to fight, but he's only one man. Neo literally has a fucking army of soldiers at his beck and call.

Not that that army did any fucking good for Theo... because he's still gone.

I should tell them, but I can't. Not yet. Telling them makes it too real. I watch the glare darken Neo's face as his eyes narrow. He doesn't like being threatened, but this is the one time I need him to let it go. "Neo, no. They're family," I warn.

He glances over to me before smirking. "Sure, boss, whatever you say." Then he turns and walks towards the kitchen with a confused-looking Bray following close behind.

Chapter Two

Holly

"**H**ol, I get that you really liked this guy, and I can see that you're hurting. But you will be okay. You can come home with us. It will be okay. You'll get through this." Reilly brushes her hands through my hair.

"No, you don't understand. He wasn't just some

guy I fancied, Rye. I love him. I... he... we got married last week. We were meant to have a lifetime together." I hold up my left hand, staring at the ring that held so many promises. The future of being his. *A future he's no longer a part of.*

Reilly snatches my wrist and drags it up to her face. "What the fuck, Hol? You married him? And you didn't tell me? Why the bloody hell wouldn't you tell me? And why would you marry someone you've only known for a couple of weeks. This is insane! What the actual fuck?" By the time she finishes her rant, she's pacing around the room and waving her arms in the air. Reilly is nothing if not overly dramatic.

"I love him. I can't explain it, but he's it for me, Reilly. I need him back. I need him to come back. He promised we would have a lifetime of memories together." My eyes are sore from crying. I can't do this anymore. I need to escape... I just don't know how. I need numbness. I need to not feel *this* anymore.

Bray walks back into the room and stares at me in a way I've never seen before. I can't decipher the look on his face. "Babe, can you go fix Holly a drink in the kitchen? Maybe something to eat too." He doesn't look at Reilly but continues to stare at me.

"What? Bray, she bloody married him! She's married, and we didn't know. Wait, did you even have a dress? Oh my God, I didn't get to help pick your dress," she rambles on.

"We were going to have a big ceremony next year,"

I whisper. I hate to admit it, but I was already planning things in my head.

"Babe, food, drink," Bray says again, snapping Reilly out of her own thoughts.

She glances between me and her husband. "Sure, I'll get you a sandwich." I don't bother to tell her I won't eat it anyway. I haven't been able to get much down the last few days.

Bray silently sits down in front of me. "Holly, sweetheart, please, *for the love of God,* tell me you're not thinking about hurting yourself. You can't do that to us. I know you're hurting right now and you feel like that might be the answer. But it's not."

I look behind me. Bloody Neo. Even though I don't know where he is, I know he told Bray about that little glass incident. "I-I wasn't. I don't know. I can't handle this pain, Bray. I just wanted the pain to stop."

"I know, sweetheart, but you can't do *that.* Think of what it would do to your family. To us. To Reilly."

"I know. I'm sorry. I just... I can't."

"Promise me that you'll talk to me, talk to me if you ever feel like that again. I won't judge. I will stay with you for as long as it takes. I just need you to not do anything that can't be undone."

"Okay. I won't. It was a passing thought."

"We're going to help you get through this, Hol. We will do whatever you need us to do."

"Thank you," I choke out. I'm glad my sister has

him. He's probably one of the best people I've ever met. He's loyal, and he'll do anything for Reilly.

T would have done anything for me too. He said all I had to do was ask. That gives me an idea... *All I have to do is ask.*

I jump up. Bray watches me as I walk down the hall and head back to the bedroom. I need to find my phone. *All I have to do is ask,* I repeat the thought.

I'm rummaging through my bag when Neo knocks at my door. I pull out my phone. It's dead—of course it is. I haven't bothered to look at it for three days.

"Holly, I need to head out for a few hours. Will you be okay here with your sister and brother-in-law?" My heart stops.

I didn't realize how much I was leaning on Neo. What if he doesn't return? "Will—will you come back?" I ask. He has his own home after all. He has his own life, and I'm sure I've taken up more of his time than I should.

"Yes, I'll be back. I've had the guest room next to this one made up for your sister. Here, take this." He holds out a small handgun. "Remember: shoot first, ask questions later. If need be... But if anything happens, you know where to go."

I look to the closet. There's a safe room at the back. T made sure I knew how to access it. "Why would I need this?" I ask.

"You won't. It's a precaution. You're the queen of

the Valentino family, Holly. Don't forget that. You bow down to no one. *Ever*."

I shake my head. What's a queen without her king? Right now? Vengeful—*that's what she is*. "Are you going to look for whoever did this?" I ask.

"Yes. I gotta go. I'll be back soon. Try to sleep some." Neo kisses my forehead before walking out the door. I put the gun in the bedside table and plug my phone into the charger.

"Holly, I got you a sandwich." Reilly walks into the room and looks around. I know she's worried about me. I don't want to make her worry, but what am I meant to do? Pretend that I'm okay? I don't know how to do that.

I take the plate from her. "Thanks." Setting the plate on the table, I turn towards the bathroom. "I think I'll just have a shower first."

"Good idea. I wasn't going to say anything, but you really bloody stink, woman. Go jump in the shower, and I'll find you some clothes," she says.

"Okay." I can give her that. She needs to feel useful, and if picking out some clothes for me to wear is what's going to do that, I'll let her.

The hot water scalds my skin. I don't bother adjusting the temperature. I need this. I need the heat. I squirt some of T's shampoo into my hands and comb it through my hair. I lather myself with his bodywash. The scent is both soothing and heart-wrenching

Reilly barges into the bathroom. "Okay, I get why you married this guy. That wardrobe, Hol, it's literally the best thing I've ever seen." *Of course she would love his wardrobe.* "I found you a shirt and some yoga pants," she says, making herself comfortable on the side of the tub. I guess she's staying? Did Bray or Neo tell her about the glass? I really hope they're not going to watch me around the clock now. It was a moment of weakness. I don't know if I would have done it anyway. Right now, the only thing I can think about is finding a way to get Theo back. I have to believe he's coming back.

I wonder how his mother is doing... I haven't seen or spoken to her, but maybe I should pay her a visit today or tomorrow. I don't even know what time it is... I've completely lost track.

I turn the water off and grab the towel Reilly hands me. Wrapping myself in the fluffy white cotton, I tug on the yoga pants she found. Then I hold up the shirt and toss it aside. Walking into the closet, I pull out another one of T's white business shirts. I need to feel him.

"Well, I guess that works too," Reilly says as she stands in the doorway, watching me.

Chapter Three

Holly

It's three in the morning, and I'm sitting here, holding my phone in my hands. I have T's text history up. I've typed in a message over and over, only to delete it again. What if I'm wrong? What if he doesn't answer? What if he really is gone? Am I clinging to a hope that's no more than a fantasy? I type in a message again.

Me: I need you to come back. I can't do this anymore. It hurts too much. Please come back, T.

I press send and watch the screen. I see the *read* tick on the message. Someone has viewed the text. Then there are those three little dots—like *that someone* is typing a reply—before they disappear. *Someone* read my message. *T* read my message. I try a second time.

Me: Please, I love you. T? Tell me you're coming back.

Again, I wait. And again, the message has been read. Whether it's Theo or not, someone has his phone. I should tell Neo... But I have this feeling he's hiding something from me. Maybe he knows where Theo is after all. If this is just some sick game of theirs, I'm going to kill them both.

I leap to my feet and tiptoe to the living room. I dig through the drawers on the table until I find T's keys for that fancy car of his. I know it's early, but if *I* can't sleep, I know there is one other person who won't be sleeping either. She may not like me very much, but I need someone who won't bullshit me. And she's the only one I can think of. Before I can talk myself out of it, I press the button for the lift. It opens with two burly men inside.

"Mrs. Valentino," they greet me politely.

"Morning." I offer them a tight smile. Are they going to stop me from leaving? Then I remember Neo's words: *you're the queen*.

So, I act like the queen I very much don't feel like at the moment. "I need to go and see my mother-in-law. Which one of you would like to follow me?" I smirk.

They glance between each other before they nod. "We both will, ma'am. We can drive you over to the estate," one of them says, pressing the button on the lift to go to the basement.

"That won't be necessary. I like driving. What are your names?" I question.

"I'm Sean. And this is Peter, ma'am."

"It's nice to meet you, Sean, Peter." I exit the lift and press the key fob to unlock the car. "Try to keep up... if you can." I smile politely as I close myself into the vehicle. *This* is what I need. I need to feel *this*. Freedom. Before I reverse, I decide to try to get a response one more time.

Me: Just so you know, I'm taking your car. I'm going to break every traffic rule, and you'll probably get loads of fines.

Just like the first two, the message is read. But no response. I press my foot down and feel the rumble of the engine. I don't even make it out of the garage before my phone is ringing through the speakers of the car. I answer it quickly. "T?"

"No, Holly, it's Neo. What the fuck are you doing? Where are you going?" He growls into the receiver.

"Sorry, I can't hear you—*bad connection*," I say. Now, I'm more convinced than ever that he knows where my husband is. T isn't dead. He can't be.

"Don't you dare fucking hang..." Oh, but I do dare. *Click.* I'm tempted to turn my phone off, but I don't, on the off-chance T calls or messages me back.

Fifteen minutes later, I pull up to the gates of his parents' estate. I wind down my window and smile at the guard. "Good morning. How are you today?"

He looks baffled by my question but silently smiles back and presses the button to let me in. Huh, this *being Mrs. Valentino* thing really does get doors opened for you.

I stop in front of the ridiculously huge steps and climb out of the car. Taking a deep breath, I look behind me but don't see the SUV with Peter and Sean —I guess they couldn't keep up after all. Then, straightening my shoulders, I ascend the stairs. The doors swing open as I get to the top.

"Mrs. Valentino, how are you?" The housekeeper greets me.

"I've been better. How are you, Teresa?"

She looks taken aback that I remember her name, but she recovers quickly. "Same. Please come in. Mrs. Valentino is in the library."

"She's awake?"

"She hasn't really been to sleep."

I follow the petite woman to the library and find Gloria with a glass of wine. She looks terrible... I'm second-guessing coming here now. Nerves fill my stomach. But I need answers.

"Gloria, it's me... Holly," I say as I approach. Her eyes are just as red-rimmed and puffy as my own. And I can't help but burst into tears the moment we make eye contact.

"Holly, it's three in the morning... What are you doing driving around at this hour?"

"I-I don't know. I needed to speak with you. I don't know what else to do. I don't know how to do this. Everything is wrong."

"I've lost my husband and son within weeks of each other. I'm not going to be of much help to you," she dismisses me.

"I'm sorry. I shouldn't have come. It's just... I... What if he wasn't in that building? What if T wasn't there?"

She looks up, waiting for me to say more. So, I blurt out everything, every little inconsistency—every hope —that I've had over the last three days, ending with the viewed text messages from his phone. "Someone has his phone?" she reiterates.

"Yes, look. I sent these tonight. Someone has read them." I hand her the device. "Why would he do this, Gloria? Why would he leave me like this?" I ask with tears running down my face.

"You really love my son, don't you?" It's an observation, not a question.

"I love him more than I ever thought I could love anyone. I need him to be okay. I need him to come home."

"Have you tried calling the number?" she prompts.

I shake my head no. "Who would have his phone? If it's not him, who?"

"I don't know. Theo was very paranoid and careful when it came to security. I don't think even Neo knew how to get into his phone."

"Then why is someone reading the messages? I don't get it. Is it possible he's still alive?" I can hear the desperation in my own voice.

"I knew something was off. Those fucking assholes. Whatever it is they're up to, they won't tell us about it. If there is a reason Theo wanted us to think he's dead, then we need to go along with it, Holly. We can't mess up whatever bullshit plan they've concocted."

"How am I meant to do that? I just need to know. I just need a sign."

"This is your sign. He's reading your messages. Come on, you look exhausted. Let me set you up in T's old room."

"I-I haven't been able to sleep."

"Me either. Thank you for coming here. I needed this." Gloria tugs me into a hug and leads me upstairs. I walk in and instantly smell T. It's like he's been here recently, but I know that's impossible. "Rest, and we'll talk over breakfast. We still have to go ahead with the service. Father Thomas will be here for lunch tomorrow."

"You're planning a service for T?" I choke out.

"We have to. It's what we'd do normally... if he were really gone."

"Do you believe he's still alive? Am I crazy?" I ask.

"I believe there's a chance he is. And I'll cling to that chance just as much as you are."

"Thank you."

Gloria nods her head and shuts the door. I walk around the room before I decide to lie down on his bed. I wonder how long it's been since T has slept in it? The room looks untouched. His mother obviously hasn't altered a thing since he moved out.

I wake with a start. A hand covers my face. I immediately throw my elbow back behind me, and whoever has a grip on my mouth lets go with an Italian expletive. It only takes a second before my brain registers the voice. I jump out of bed and pounce on my would-be attacker.

"T?" I ask. "What the bloody hell?" I punch him in the shoulder.

"Ow, fuck, dolcezza. Shhh. I need you to be quiet," he says.

Be quiet? Is he bloody serious? I'm going to strangle him. I laugh—it's a maniacal laugh. "You have to be kidding me. Where the hell have you been?" I ask with venom in my voice. I'm angry, I'm relieved, and I'm terrified of his answer.

"I'm sorry. I'm so sorry, dolcezza. But I can't stay long. I just... I couldn't keep away..."

"What do you mean you *can't stay*? What's going on, T? Where have you been?"

Chapter Four

Three days earlier

"Y"ou know this is a fucked-up plan. It's probably not gonna work," Neo says.

"I know, but what choice do we have? Just do your part. And make sure she's okay." I send up a silent prayer, hoping that Holly will forgive me for what I'm about to put her through. I can't see any other way around this fucking problem though.

"Fine. But when she kicks your ass to the curb, don't tell me I didn't warn you."

I watch as Neo drives off. He's heading to the school to pick up Holly. I need her to see it with her own eyes... to believe that I'm really gone. So she doesn't do anything rash and put herself in danger.

I've found a spot in the bushes with a clear sight-line of the building, when the idea of how to kill two birds with one stone crosses my mind. Probably not my smartest move, but I'm "dying" anyway. What have I got to lose?

I send a message, asking *him* to meet me at this address. Ten minutes later, I watch as he pulls up with four of his men. They enter the building while scanning their surroundings. *Yeah, you should be on edge, motherfucker.* You fucking touched what's mine. It's time you paid the price.

Neo and I rigged the building to blow—there're explosives in every room. All set to go off with the flick of a button. A button I control.

I place a call to my second, telling him I need that package I left in his car. He hates this plan. I don't fucking like it either. But it's not until I see him pull up, with Holly in the passenger seat, that the doubt really takes hold. My heart stops when she gets out of the car. I can't let her near that building. Without thinking, I press the button and watch Neo tackle her to the ground. But it's what I see next—Holly's reaction—that truly fucking breaks me. I've never regretted anything before. But this? Putting *this* on her... I fucking hate myself.

I wait until Neo has her back in his car and is driving away before I move. Within the hour, everyone in New York will hear of my demise. And I'll become the ghost I need to be to get this shit done.

At least one obstacle (that fucking bastard—John Junior) is removed from the picture now. There's no way he or his men made it out of that building. They'll be searching for identifiable body parts for months after this, and they still won't be able to piece the man back together. He never should have threatened Holly. Because when he did, he fucking sealed his fate, along with those of the men he brought with him.

I slink along the back alleyway and jump into the car I parked here earlier. It's a piece of shit, and nothing like the luxury vehicles I'm used to driving. I shed my tailor-made suit and put on the jeans and plain black tee Neo picked up for me. It's time to reinvent myself. To become the low-level thug no one would suspect.

Turning into the center of Hell's Kitchen, I cruise by the strip club the three bosses told me about. This is where they hold the auctions, selling off the fucking women and kids they've abducted. I have a contact. Paulie. He's a guard on the premises. He got me a job working the door. It's not the best vantage point. But a lot gets said on the sidewalk, and I'll also be able to see every fucker walking in.

I park the car, slide on a worn-in leather jacket, light a cigarette, and stroll across the street like I belong. No one would expect Theo Valentino to be in a place like this; no one would expect *him* to work a shitty bouncer job at a dingy-ass strip joint either. That's what I'm fucking hoping anyway.

"You're late," Paulie says as I approach the red rope.

I shrug my shoulders. "Got held up."

"Don't make it a fucking habit." He smirks. Usually, I'd throw an uppercut his way for speaking to me like that. I clench and unclench my fist. I need to let it go. I'm not *me* right now. I have a job to do. And the quicker I do it, the quicker I can get back to my wife. I do, however, raise an eyebrow at the cocky bastard. He's the only one here who knows the truth about me. I know he's loyal to my family—loyal to a fucking fault. My father picked him up off the streets and gave the kid a job when no one else would.

"Just tell me what to do," I grunt.

"Stand here. Check IDs. Don't let too many minors in. That's it."

"Okay."

Paulie walks away, shaking his head. "Good luck," he throws over his shoulder. What the fuck do I need luck for? I'm standing at a door, checking fucking IDs. It's not rocket science.

Three hours into my so-called shift, I finally got something. A face I can put a name to. They don't know who I am, but I sure as fuck know who *they* are. Noah Kelly, AKA one nasty Irish motherfucker. It doesn't surprise me to find the son of a bitch involved in this shitshow. He's as dirty and fucking sick as they come.

He's also fucking stupid. He and his pathetic posse walked straight past me, not an ounce of recognition. If they looked up long enough to engage in a proper greeting, I'm sure the dumbasses would have spotted me.

I pull out my burner phone and fire off a message to the other three.

Me: Problem one: blown-away by our proposition. Next problem: four-leaf clover.

Within seconds, the phone beeps with their replies.

B1: I heard. Not impressed by your choice. Keep tabs on the Clover.

B2: Good-fucking-riddance, I say. Well done, son. Be careful. The Clover may look stupid, but don't underestimate him.

B3: For fuck's sake, T, don't rush into anything. We want to know the entire

spread. Get the Clover. Do whatever you have to, to get the info out of him.

I shake my head. They've turned into the fucking *Mob Wives* of New York or some shit. Seriously, who the fuck put these names into my burner?

Me: B1, B2, B3, fuck you all. Whoever thought that shit up needs a bullet between the eyes and a shallow grave.

B2: Focus on the job, T.

Me: Aye, Aye, captain.

I turn the phone off and try to decipher who's who. It's not hard, judging by the tone of each message. It also doesn't fucking matter. What does matter? Figuring out a way inside and getting as close as I can to the Clover.

For two hours, I sat at the bar and nursed the same fucking glass of whisky. From my vantage point, I could fucking hear everything too. I know when the next auction is, I know who's running it, and I know where the cargo is being held.

Ever heard the phrase: *loose lips sink ships*? Well, those loose lips of Noah Kelly's just sent him sinking like the goddamn Titanic. I'm also hoping this new information will help put an end to this double-life bullshit. And I'll be able to get back to Holly sooner.

I get up, throw a twenty down on the bar, and walk out. I won't be back. I can't risk being seen here twice—on the off-chance someone did spot me.

Lying on the shitty fucking bed, in the shitty fucking apartment Neo found for me, I fire off a text to him.

Me: How is she?

Neo: I fucking hate you right now. I've never seen someone more broken than she is. And I've broken a lot of fucking people.

Fuck! I punch the wall and embrace the sting to my knuckles. I need the pain. I need something. I don't bother texting him back. What the fuck would I say anyway? Right now, my best friend, my cousin, is comforting my grieving wife. *My fucking wife*. My blood boils at the irrational thought of him getting too close to her. And I'm fucking pissed that I've pushed them together. He's the only one I trust to keep her safe. But can I really trust him to keep his fucking hands off her at the same time?

I shake my head. *Of course I can.* Neo would never fucking betray me like that.

Chapter Five

One day earlier

I'm at the docks, where Noah Kelly said the shipment would be. My plan was to just watch the bastards unload, then tail them. That *was* the plan, until I saw the contents of the shipment.

I call the number saved as B1 in my phone. I expect Hal to answer—he's the head of the Gambino family. At least I'm hoping it's him. Out of the three, he's the most tolerable. It's not him though. It's Leo Lambourne instead. "T, what you got?" he answers.

"I'm down at the docks. Leo, this is fucked up. These girls can't be older than eight."

"Okay. But you know what you have to do: *follow 'em and wait for backup*. Do not go in alone."

"This is bigger than we thought, Leo. These girls, they're all Italian. I'm sending you a picture now—the guy's walking around here like his shit don't stink. I don't know who the fuck he is. I've never seen him before."

"Got it. Fuck me. T, don't fucking do anything. Get the fuck out of there. *Now*. Go to the meet-up place. We'll see you there."

"No, we need to know where they're taking these girls."

"No, you need to do as you're told, kid. That bastard in the photo, that's Big Harry. We need to reevaluate this plan."

"The plan stays. I don't care who the fuck this Big Harry thinks he is." I hang up. I've heard rumors about the fucker—he's some drug lord over in Italy. I've just never really cared enough to learn anything else about him. I guess I probably should have. I fire off a text to Neo.

Me: Who and what is Big Harry?

Neo calls instead of messaging back. "Where are you?"

"At the docks. Who's this Big Harry bastard?" I'm starting to get impatient. I want some fucking answers.

"He's a fucking psychotic loose cannon. I've heard he eats his kills. *Hannibal Lector style*, T. Whatever you do, stay the fuck away from him."

"Why is everyone so scared of this guy?" I ask. I don't get it.

"Actually, I don't know. But I sure as fuck want this whole shit to end sooner rather than later, because your wife needs you to come fucking home."

"How's she doing?" I prompt.

"How do you think she's doing? She thinks the love of her life just got blown to pieces. She's a fucking mess, man. I can't get her to eat. She barely sleeps. And when she does, she wakes up screaming."

"Did you get her sister here?" I don't know how to help her. I wish I could just tell her the truth... that I'm okay. But I need this shit to be believable. I need a grieving widow.

"Yeah, she should be arriving tomorrow."

"Good. I gotta go. Just try to make sure she eats something." My gut is wrenching. I feel like absolute fucking shit for having to do this to her. I've almost caved over and over again the last two days, wanting to send her a message, or reach out via text. *Something*. Anything to let her know not to give up on us.

She has to know there's still an *us*. Our story is far from done.

Pulling out my phone, I snap a photo of the building and take note of the address. I followed the trucks here —the trucks full of fucking young Italian girls. This is fucked up. I want to go in there on a killing spree. I'd love to watch their blood spill, put an end to each one of those sick bastards.

I try to think of what my father would have done. I can't believe he'd have known about this. There is no way he would stand by and allow this to happen to a bunch of kids. Not after what happened to Lola, my cousin and Neo's younger sister. She disappeared when she was nine. The family never even found so much as a trace of her whereabouts. It makes me sick to my stomach to think that *this* could have been her fate. I shake the thoughts from my head. I can't lose focus now.

I drive over to the meeting place. The others are already there by the time I pull up. "Where the fuck have you been? You do realize I've got other shit to deal with?" Leo grunts.

"Yeah, so the fuck do I, asshole. At least all of you fuckers get to go home to your wives tonight," I reply. They drop their eyes, unable to meet mine. Bastards. "What aren't you fucking telling me?"

"We need you to go to Italy," Hal says. "Big Harry is involved, which means this is bigger than we thought. It's bigger than just the New York families. We want this ring shut down. I've spoken to Al Donatello. He's on board. Whatever you need over there—whatever you can't source yourself—he'll help you get."

Al Donatello, you might as well call him the fucking *King of Kings*. He rules the whole of the Italian underworld. If he's backing us, then why the fuck isn't he doing the dirty work himself? "Why doesn't Donatello just shut it down? He has boots on the ground."

"He suspects he has a rat. He wants you to infiltrate his crew, spend time getting to know them, and find out who's eating cheese. Should be easy enough."

Yeah, a piece of fucking cake. "You know what? I don't need this shit. I have businesses to run. I have a fucking family here that needs me to do shit too. Hire another exterminator for your *rat problem*." I turn to walk away. I'll figure out how to free those girls myself. I'm not going to fucking Italy.

"You know, we were prepared to look the other way, when you let Lana get off with not so much as a slap on the wrist... after killing *two* Dons. But maybe we should bring it to the attention of the council. I'm sure they'll have something to say about it," Leo comments.

My steps falter. Fucking fuckers. "I don't know

what you're talking about." I fold my arms over my chest.

"Sure you don't," Hal adds. "We let it go, because that piece of shit she called a father deserved what he got. Your pops, not so much." He shrugs.

"Fine, I'll go to fucking Italy. I'll give it two weeks. If I can't get the information in that time, I'm out."

"Fine, I'm sure it won't take that long anyway," Leo agrees. "A ghost can haunt places us regular guys can't."

I storm off, wondering if this was their plan all along and why I needed to *die*. To get whatever information they wanted from Italy. I'm not buying into the bullshit about Al Donatello needing someone to find a rat. He'd be able to get that shit done within his own family. Something else is off here. I just don't know what. And until I figure it out, I need to go along with their plans.

I head back to the shitty apartment.

I'm lying on the bed. I have no idea what time it is, but something urges me to log into the cameras in my penthouse. I've avoided doing so for the past two days. I want to see her. But I know if I do, I'll want more—like that kid story about giving a mouse a cookie and shit—

and I can't give into my impulses right now. It won't benefit either of us in the long run.

I load the servers and search through the kitchen and living areas. They're empty. I check the bedroom, and I see her sleeping on the chair. It's dark, so I can't make out her features. Why isn't she in bed?

She wakes with a start and jumps up. It looks like she's yelling at something... or someone? But there's no one else there. I shouldn't do it, but I do. I turn the sound up so I can hear what she's saying. "When? When the hell are you coming back?"

Fuck, my heart shatters. I hate that I'm doing this to her. I will fucking never forgive myself... I can't fucking stand seeing her so torn up. Then she chucks a glass against the wall. *Let it out, dolcezza. Trash the whole fucking room if you need to.*

I watch as she falls to the ground, picks up a shard, and stares at it. "I just want the pain to go away," she cries.

"NO!" I scream. *No fucking way.* I call Neo. "Get to Holly. Now, Neo. Fucking stop her!" I yell into the receiver when he picks up. I hold my breath for the thirty seconds it takes him to appear on screen as he rushes into my bedroom. Holly looks up at him in shock. He takes the glass out of her hands. *Thank fuck...* I have to do something. I can't let her keep believing I'm dead. What was I fucking thinking? That she'd cry for a day or two, mourn a little bit, but that she'd ultimately be okay?

Not fucking likely. This is the girl who willingly held a gun to a mob boss's head, without flinching, to make sure I was safe. Of course she's not going to be okay with thinking I'm dead.

I watch Neo pick her up, and my jaw clenches. *That* should be me. I should be there with her. No, she shouldn't be so broken-hearted in the first place. He takes her out to the kitchen. I turn the cameras off. She's safe now. He won't leave her alone again.

My phone beeps with a new message.

Neo: I don't know what to do here, T. She was literally going to cut herself in there. You need to put an end to this.

Me: I know. Just… don't leave her alone. I'll fix this.

He doesn't respond. I don't need him to. I know he won't let me down.

Chapter Six

It's been a few hours since I watched Holly contemplate the unthinkable. My skin is itching to go and see her, to put her out of this fucked-up misery. I'm second-guessing everything the other three bosses have said to me over the last few days. Is she really safe here? What happens if I get on a plane to Italy and leave her behind? She'll be alone. She'll be surrounded by as many men as I can possibly get, but she'll still be *alone*.

Fuck that. I'm not leaving New York like this. But I can't take her with me either. I can't fathom the mess I'll be walking into out there. And there's no way I want Holly dragged into that shitshow.

My brain is whirling with every possible idea and scenario of how best to protect her. To protect my whole fucking family, the empire my forefathers built. I won't fail them. Any of them. I will show these assholes that I may be young, but that doesn't mean I'm stupid. Whatever plans are in the works against me and mine, they'll regret it. Whoever the fuck *they* are.

I have to get Lana out. She needs to be hidden... somewhere no one can find her. I don't trust anyone. Those fuckers know she's responsible for killing both of our fathers. I haven't forgiven her in the least, but I can't sit by and watch her in front of the firing squad either. I won't talk to her. I can't. But I know someone who would do anything for that woman. I flick through my contacts until I have the number. Alexei Petrov. "Yeah?" he answers.

"I need a favor." I hate the fucking words, even as I say them.

"Yeah, most people do. Who the fuck are you, and what do you want?" he growls.

"It's not for me. And if I had another way, I wouldn't be fucking asking your ass. It's about Lana." I pause, hearing his sharp intake of breath. So, *now* I got your attention, motherfucker.

"I'm listening."

"You need to get her out of town. They know. Tell her they all fucking know what she did. She needs to go before they find her."

"Woah, hold the fuck up! What are you talking about? What are you accusing her of? And who are *they*?"

"Maybe you should be asking her that. I thought she trusted you and your people. Or better yet, ask her friend Elena. Ask her what the fuck she gave to Lana, and what she told her she could do with it." I let my rage overtake me for a moment. "Look, just get her out of town for a bit. I'll call back when it's safe for her to come home."

"You still haven't told me who the fuck you are, and why I should be listening to you."

"You're right. I haven't." I hang up. I've seen him around Lana. I know he won't take the risk. As prideful as the fucker is, he'll listen to me and get her to leave the city, or at least hide her out in one of their fucking Russian safe houses. No one knows she's fucking a Russian—except me. At least I fucking hope no one else knows. I throw myself back on the bed when the phone beeps in my hand. I open it, not even thinking twice.

Holly: I need you to come back. I can't

do this anymore. It hurts too much. Please come back, T.

I start typing a reply to her, to tell her that I'll come home. That it's all going to be okay. But I delete the words before I can send them. A minute later, another text arrives.

Holly: Please, I love you. T? Tell me you're coming back.

I read the message but can't respond. What am I supposed to do here? She fucking needs me. I fucking need her. This whole fake death shit is just that: *fucking shit.* I don't want her to hurt... I can't sit by and watch her like this. About ten minutes later, a new message appears.

Holly: Just so you know, I'm taking your car. I'm going to break every traffic rule, and you'll probably get loads of fines.

Fuck! She's being fucking reckless. She thinks she has nothing to live for anymore. She doesn't care if she hurts herself. Fuck! I stand and throw on my jeans and a shirt. Then I call Neo. He's doing a shit job right now. "Boss?" he answers.

"Where are you, and why the fuck is Holly taking my car out for a goddamn joyride?" I scream down the phone, already descending the five flights of stairs to get to the entrance of this decrepit apartment building.

"Ah, I had some errands. Her sister and brother-in-law were with her. I made sure they wouldn't leave her alone. Fuck, hold on." I wait, listening as he taps away on the keyboard.

"She's, ah, heading to your parents' place. She just put the address into the navigation."

"Call her and tell her to go back upstairs." He uses a different phone to call her. He has her on speaker, and hearing her voice is fucking torture. Especially when she's still holding out hope that it's me on the other end of that line. She answers by whispering my name.

"Well, fuck, she fucking hung up on me." Neo's shock is clear.

"I'm sure it's not the first time you've been hung up on," I say dryly. I'm jogging to my beater car.

"Well, yeah, but I thought we were friends. Want me to follow her to your parents?"

"Like you'd be able to keep up with her crazy fucking back-street, bullshit driving. I told you not to let her out of your sight. And why the fuck is she visiting my mother at three in the goddamn morning?"

"No idea. I'll call ahead, to make sure the guards know to let her in. I'll meet her there and bring her back to your place," he offers.

"Don't bother. I'm almost there."

I park the car across the street (out of sight) and jog down under the trees, keeping to the shadows. The best thing about breaking into your own estate: you know where every fucking camera and guard are stationed. I never had a reason to sneak in and out before. I pretty much did whatever I wanted growing up. My parents didn't care as long as I was always there for Sunday dinner and kept up appearances.

Well, fuck... I wasn't planning on running into anyone back here. My father was one fucking thorough bastard—that's for sure. I watch for a bit and note that each guard changes places every five minutes. I figured if I try to jump this fence, I'll be shot before any of the idiots realize it's me. My best bet is to go around the front. Either knock out the guard at the gate, or threaten him enough that he won't speak a word of my being here to anyone. I trust these men. They're all loyal. I just don't want to fuck up this plan before I've determined what the other bosses are up to.

Jogging around the front, I trudge up to the gate. And I have two barrels pointed at my head before I make it within ten feet of the iron bars. "You may want to lower those," I say, flicking my head in the direction of their guns.

"Shit, Mr. Valentino?" one of them asks.

"Yeah, long story. Don't really have time to explain. Did my wife come through earlier?"

"Yes, I let her in, boss. She's still in there, sir." He nods towards the house.

"Thank you. And I trust that you never saw me, right? Maybe you had a bad dream? Imagined something? Saw a fucking ghost... I don't care. But I was never here, got me?"

"Of course, boss. Never saw a thing."

I walk past the open gate and sneak into the house through a side door. And I'm instantly greeted by the hot end of another gun. "Fucking hell, this is happening way too fucking much tonight," I growl.

"Boss? Shit, sorry. Didn't know it was you. They said you were dead. I sure am glad you ain't."

"About that... I am. And you aren't. You're torn up —you miss me terribly and all that." I step around him and up the staircase. I creep into my old bedroom, sit on the bed, and access the security footage from my phone. This house is too fucking big. There are too many rooms to search, but I finally see her. Holly's sitting in the library with my mother. It looks like they're crying. Fuck... I'm going to hell for this.

They both stand, and my mother hugs Holly before leading her out. I follow, on camera, as they climb the stairs. It's not until they're standing outside the fucking door that I realize my mother is bringing her *here*. Why the fuck would she bring Holly to my old bedroom? This house has ten guest rooms. I jump into the closet and turn my phone off. The light comes on, and my mother tells Holly to get some rest, then mentions some shit about planning my memorial service tomorrow. There's enough illumination that I can see Holly looking around. She sighs and curls up on the bed. It's not long before she's sleeping. I open the door and peer down at her. I can't walk away without letting her know that it's going to be okay.

I thought waking her up with my palm over her mouth was a good idea... right up until I catch an elbow to the chest. "Fuck," I groan.

"T? What the bloody hell?" She follows it with a jab to my shoulder.

"Ow, fuck, dolcezza. Shhh. I need you to be quiet," I urge.

Then she laughs, but not joyously. No, this is different. It's like she's lost her goddamn mind. "You have to be kidding me. Where the hell have you been?" She's pissed...

"I'm sorry. I'm so sorry, dolcezza. But I can't stay long. I just... I couldn't keep away..."

"What do you mean you *can't stay*? What's going on, T? Where have you been?"

I clearly didn't think this through. What the fuck am I gonna tell her? Instead of answering her questions, I do what I've been dreaming about doing for the last three fucking days. I slam my lips down on hers. I push my tongue inside her mouth, and I take everything she has to give me. I greedily find comfort in this kiss, when I'm the one who should be comforting her. I pick her up, throw her back onto the bed, and land on top of her. "I fucking missed you."

"Why? Why did you do this to me?" she asks, her voice wavering.

"I'll tell you when I can. I promise. Just not yet." I lean down and fuse our lips together again. Sliding my hand under the shirt she's wearing, I palm her breast and twist her nipple. Her back arches off the bed, pressing her chest into mine, and her legs wrap around my waist as she clings to me. "I fucking love you, Holly. I'll always come back to you. Don't you fucking forget that." My mouth makes its way down her neck.

"I thought I lost you. I... it was too much, Theo," she cries. And I wipe the tears from her cheeks with my thumb.

"I know. I'm sorry. I'm so fucking sorry." I rest my forehead on hers. We're both breathing heavily. I sit up and pull her yoga pants down her legs, before ripping the shirt open. Then I lie back and tug her on top of me. "I need to see you. I need to see you, Holly."

She nods her head and bites her bottom lip. Her hands are trembling as she undoes my belt and jeans, freeing my raging fucking hard-on. The moment her soft palm wraps around my shaft, I lose all inhibitions.

"I need to be inside you now. I need to fucking feel your pussy milk my cock, dolcezza. Are you wet for me, Holly?" I ask, knowing full well that she is. She always fucking is. She nods her head and settles herself at the tip of my cock, slowly sliding on to the length. "Fuck! I fucking need you," I say, holding her hips as I push her all the way down until she bottoms out.

"Oh, God, Theo, yes. Oh, God." Her moans get louder. And at this point, I don't care who fucking hears her. I want the world to know that she's mine, that I do *this* to her. No one fucking else.

"You're fucking perfect. My queen. My everything." I raise her hips before slamming her back down again. She feels so fucking good. I know if I don't hold back, I'm going to come way too fucking fast. I don't want this to be over yet. I reach up and palm her breasts. Her hands rest on my chest as she slowly circles her pussy around my cock.

"Don't leave me again," she whispers as she leans forward to cup my face. "I can't do this life without you, T. Don't fucking leave me again. Please." She's begging me...

I want to tell her that I won't. But this is the fucking mafia. I can't guarantee a tomorrow. All I can promise is that I'll do everything in my power to be there each morning when she opens her eyes. That I'll be the first thing she sees when she wakes up, and the last thing she sees before she goes to bed at night.

Chapter Seven

Holly

Theo rolls us over so he's on top. He's actually here. He's inside me. His hands are on me. His mouth is on me. *If this is a dream, please, God, I don't want to wake up.* Let me have this forever. I'll do anything. Just let it be real...

Theo sits up and pulls my legs over his shoulders. Holding my ankles, he starts to thrust into me, hard and fast.

"Fuck. Oh, God. Don't stop. Don't ever stop." My thoughts are chaotic, but one thing is crystal-clear, and that's the orgasm I'm chasing. I'm so close.

"Fucking come for me, Holly. I need you to come for me now," T demands, right before he bites into my ankle.

"Ow, fuck!" I fall over the cliff. And T follows, his body jolting as the warm liquid squirts inside me. He collapses on the bed and pulls me against him, his hand curled around me and his fingertips twirling the ends of my hair. "Please tell me this isn't a dream. Tell me you're real." My voice quivers at the thought of waking up and realizing he's gone.

"It's not a dream, dolcezza." T's voice is rough, his chest still heaving.

I lie there, wrapped in his arms. I want to ask where he's been. I want to ask how he could do this to me. There are so many questions running through my mind. But most of all, I don't want to ask anything... just enjoy the silence and his embrace. This is my happy place, my sanctuary. I can hear the clock on the wall ticking by, almost like it's taunting me. Are we on borrowed time? How long will it be before he's gone again? He may not have died in that building. But this life he leads... it's dangerous, and the possibility of him not coming home to me is higher than I'd like to admit.

I sit, untangling myself from his hold. I *do* need answers. I can't be the docile housewife who just accepts everything for what it is. I can't live with all these doubts in my head. "Where were you?" I ask, pulling the sheet up and over my chest.

"I was working. I can't tell you what I was doing, dolcezza. I don't want to put you in any more danger than I already have by bringing you into this world in the first place." He reaches his hand out for me. I shimmy backwards.

I won't let his touch interfere with my judgement. "No, you *won't* tell me. *Can't* and *won't* are two different things, Theo. W-were you with someone else? Oh my God, were you with another woman?" My voice rises and my eyes sting.

Theo's face hardens, his jaw tenses, and his gaze darkens. "Absolutely fucking not. Fuck, Holly, you think I'd cheat on you? No, never. I swear to you there was not *and never will be* another woman."

"What else am I meant to think, Theo? You were gone for three fucking days. Three days. You let me think you were dead. I've never in my life felt a pain like that. I wanted to..." I stop my sentence there. I can't even verbalize what I was prepared to do to make the pain stop.

"I know. I'm sorry. I didn't have a choice," he says, inching closer to me.

"There's always a choice. Isn't that what you told me before? And you... you chose wrong. You broke my heart, T. *On purpose.* You said you'd never hurt me, and you did. You hurt me like no one else ever could."

"Tell me what to do. Tell me how to fix this, Holly."

"I don't think you can." I stand and walk into the bathroom. He follows, spins me around, and pushes my back against the basin. Then he throws a hand behind me and turns on the tap. "Wha—" He stops my question with a finger to his lips, before reaching into the shower and turning the water on in there too.

"I had to be a ghost. The other bosses, they showed me some pictures, a file. John Junior is... *was* involved in some really messed-up shit—shit *the families* won't stand for. I'm putting a stop to it. But in order to do that, I need to lay low. Being dead, being someone else, gives me access to information otherwise unavailable to Theo Valentino."

"What is it that you're stopping? And why does it have to be you? Can't you get someone else to do it?"

"They're selling children, Holly. Little girls, no older than fucking eight. Even if I could get someone else to do it, I want to fucking stop these sick bastards. *I have to stop it.*" His words are nothing more than a harsh whisper. But his eyes cloud over. He's determined to do his part, to save these girls. Who am I to stand here and tell him no?

"How can I help? What can I do?" I find myself asking.

"Nothing. You don't get involved in this, Holly. I need to go to Italy for a few weeks. I need you to play the grieving widow. I need people to keep thinking I'm dead."

"What? No. You're not leaving me again. Please, Theo, don't leave me again. I can't..." I'm struggling to breathe, and my chest tightens. I can feel a cold sweat forming on my skin.

"I'm not leaving you, Holly. I'm never leaving you. I just have this one job to do, then I'll be back. Two weeks, tops."

"I don't like it," I cry. I just got him back, and he's leaving again.

"Your sister's here, right? Spend some time with her. Help my mother plan a service. Actually... Ma's never been to Australia. Take her there, Holly. Send your sister back home. Get them out of New York. You will be safer over there."

"No, I'm not leaving. Take me to Italy with you." I know the request will be denied, even as I ask it, but I ask anyway.

"I can't. One day, I promise. One day, I'll take you to Italy. I'll take you to Paris. I will take you wherever you want to go. But right now, I need you to go back to Sydney. Wait for me there. Neo will accompany you."

He can't be serious? He wants me to just return to my life in Sydney and wait for him. He wants me to take Neo to Sydney. "You should have Neo with you.

You shouldn't be going into anything alone, T. This is stupid. You can't do this." I jump onto his lap and wrap myself around him.

"I have to do this, dolcezza. I need you to go home. It's just a couple of weeks. And you can't let on that you know I'm alive. After the service, get straight on the jet and go to Sydney. Please, it will be easier for me if I know that you're safe."

"Will I be able to call you? Text?" I'm desperate. Right now, I'll take any form of communication. It's better than nothing.

"I'll get you a burner. Don't use your personal phone to contact me."

I nod my head and nestle into his shoulder, inhaling his scent as it surrounds me. *It's only two weeks,* I keep telling myself. *Two weeks is nothing, when we have a lifetime to look forward to.* It will fly by. I fall back to sleep in Theo's arms, listening to his heartbeat.

"Holly, darling, I'm sorry. I didn't want to wake you, but Father Thomas will be here in an hour. I've left some clothes out. Oh, Neo is waiting downstairs with your sister and her husband. They, um, don't look too happy. Want me to send them away?" Gloria's voice rouses me from my sleep.

I sit up and look around. "Where is he? Where did he go?" I ask.

"Who?"

"Theo. Where is he?" My eyes start to water again. It felt so real. I could have sworn...

Gloria's eyes are just as tear-filled. She lowers herself on the bed and hugs me. "I'm sorry, honey. Take your time. I can tell Father Thomas to come later... if you need."

Why is she suddenly being so nice to me? This woman hated me. She wanted Theo to marry Lana not all that long ago. But now? I don't know. I don't understand it. I want to ask, but I don't want to jinx it either. I'll take the kindness, over her being cold and indifferent. "No, it's fine. I'll just have a quick shower."

"Okay." She runs her hands down my hair and inhales. "You smell like him," she says absentmindedly, before rising to her feet and walking to the door.

It was just a dream... He wasn't really here. He is gone, and I'm alone.

It's not until I'm in the shower, lathering up my legs, that I see it. A bite mark on my ankle. Holy shit... He *was* here. That really did happen. I rush through my shower, wrapping a towel around myself and heading back into the bedroom. I almost walk past it, but sitting on the dresser is a phone. No note. Nothing.

Just the phone. I power it on, and it asks for a password. I put in the first digits that come to mind: the day we signed our marriage paperwork. The phone unlocks and a message appears.

Yours: Dolcezza, use this sparingly. Remember that I love you, and that I'll always come back for you. Stick to the plan.

I type back a quick response, and a huge sense of relief washes over me.

Me: I had the best dream last night. All of my wishes came true, and I held my entire world in my arms.

I put on the dress that Gloria left out for me. It's absolutely stunning: a charcoal lace material, with a sweetheart neckline and a bodice that hugs my hips, then flares out down to my knees. The fabric feels luxurious. It's so soft. I run my fingers through my hair and position it over my shoulder. I reread the message from Theo one more time before tucking the phone into my pocket. I love this dress even more now. *It has pockets.*

It's time to face the music. I walk downstairs. I'm looking for everyone else when I run into a guard. "Mrs. Valentino." He nods his head politely in my direction.

"Hi, ah... I'm sorry, but what was your name?" I ask. It feels extremely rude, having everyone know my name when I don't know theirs.

"It's Sonnie, ma'am."

"Sonnie, good morning. Do you know where I might find my sister? Or my mother-in-law?"

"They're all in the dining room." Right, the dining room... I look from side to side. *Which way's the dining room?* "Here, let me walk you there, ma'am," Sonnie offers, realizing my confusion.

"Thank you so much." I silently follow Sonnie through the house. I like him. I have a good feeling about him. "How long have you worked here?"

"Five years, ma'am," he answers.

"You can call me Holly. I'm not old enough to be a *ma'am*. Do you have a wife? Kids?"

He looks at me with a quizzical brow. "Ah, no, I don't. Not yet."

"Ever been to Australia?" I continue.

"No, I've never been outside of New York."

"Oh, but you do have a passport? If not, how quickly could you get one?" I prompt.

"Ah, Mrs. Valentino, we can get anything we want within hours. Why? Are you in need of a passport?"

"Me? No. But I'm taking a trip back home after the service on Saturday, and I'm bringing you with me. Get a passport organized, Sonnie."

"Ah, don't take this the wrong way, Mrs. Valentino, but why me?"

I shrug. "I like you. T wouldn't want me traveling without a team of his men, so I'm taking my pick. And you're my first." I smile as I walk past him and into the dining room.

My good mood is instantly put on the backburner as three death glares turn my way.

Chapter Eight

Holly

What do they all have the shits about? I'm the one who's lost her husband. I ignore all three of them, heading for the coffee pot set out on the buffet.

"Holly, darling, come and sit. You need to eat," Gloria says.

"Thank you, Gloria. This looks lovely." I grab a seat and pile my plate with fresh fruits.

"Not to be rude, Aunt Gloria, but what the actual fuck is going on here?" Neo gestures between the older woman and me.

"Neo, language. We aren't heathens, despite your attempts to become one. Holly is my daughter. If I want to offer her breakfast, I will." Gloria puts Neo in his place. I smirk at him from across the table. "Did you drug her or something?" he asks me.

"What? No! Of course not. Don't be stupid. It really doesn't suit that pretty face of yours." I wave my fork in his direction.

Reilly, who has been otherwise silent, chokes on her toast. "Woah, hold up, Hol. That was badass. I approve."

"Thanks." I smile.

"What time is Father Thomas arriving?" I turn to Gloria.

"He should be here in about thirty minutes."

"Okay. After the service on Saturday, I'll be going home for a couple of weeks. I would love it if you'd come with me." I look over to her pleadingly. For some reason, T wants me to get his mother out of New York.

"Oh, I've never been to Australia," she ponders.

"I know. Theo told me. So, I would love to take you. Well, actually, we'll be taking one of the Valentino jets." I look to Neo. "You can arrange that for me, can't you? Oh, you're also coming along, apparently."

The intense stare Neo sends my way has me

squirming in my seat. I have no idea what he's searching for, but I know when he finds it. "Fucking idiota!" he yells.

"Neo, stop! Just get the bloody jet organized and pack your boardies. Oh, and we're taking some of the men you have around here. I'll give you a list of which."

"Holly, show me where the little girl's room is. *Now.*" Reilly stands and waits for me at the doorway. I follow her, not that I have any idea where the bathrooms are in this house. She grabs my arm and starts pulling me down the hallway.

Sonnie steps out of the shadows like a damn ninja. "I need you to remove your hands from Mrs. Valentino," he says, blocking her path.

She opens her mouth to reply, but I beat her to it. "Sonnie, this is my sister, Reilly, in case that wasn't obvious. I'm fine. *Really.* No need to worry." He glances between us but doesn't move. "Look, I really am fine. We're just searching for the bathroom. Can you point me in the right direction, please?"

"If you're sure, Mrs. Valentino. Right down that way, third door on the left."

"Great, thanks." I take hold of Reilly's hand and tug her through the hall. Once we're in the bathroom, I copy Theo's actions from last night and turn on all the taps. I have no idea why, but I do it anyway.

"Okay, who are you, and what have you done with my sister?"

"I'm still the same me, Reilly."

"No, you're not. You're way more confident. You're... I don't know... *different*. Though, not in a bad way. But what I find most intriguing is the fact that you're not sad today. You're not grieving like you were yesterday. What's changed? And what the hell is going on here? What's with the men in suits? It's like we've walked into a bad mafia movie."

"Okay, first off, I don't know why I'm more confident. Maybe it's Theo brushing off on me or something. Second, and this is really important, Rye. You can't tell anyone. Not even Bray yet. I don't want him freaking out."

"Pinkie swear I won't tell." She wiggles the digit at me, and I roll my eyes.

Then I lean in and whisper, "T isn't dead. He was here last night."

Reilly looks at me skeptically. "Okay, I believe that you *believe* that. Sometimes grief can do weird things to our brains."

"No, Rye, I'm serious. I'm not crazy. Look. Last night when we were... busy." I blush. "He bit my ankle." I show her the prominent indentation.

"Okay, say he's alive. Where is he, Hol? And why are we pretending he's dead?"

"That's the other thing. The Valentino family, they're the mafia, Reilly. That's why there're men in suits everywhere. T is kind of... the Don." I shrug.

"Shut the front door. Holly, swear to me on

Dylan's grave that you're not having me on. You did not seriously marry a bloody mob boss. My sweet, innocent, good-natured sister did not go and marry into the bloody mafia," she squeals.

"Shh, keep your voice down. You can't tell anyone. I wasn't even meant to tell you. Please, Reilly, promise me."

"Okay, I promise. But I swear to God, mob boss or not, if this husband of yours doesn't treat you like the queen you are, then I'll cut his balls off myself."

"Trust me, when you do meet him, you'll love him. He's perfect, Reilly—well, except for the whole making me think he was dead part. But he had his reasons, and we need to act like we don't know he's still alive. We're going to do the service and then go back to Sydney for a few weeks."

"Holly, are you really sure about this? I mean, the mafia? People get like tortured and end up in jail and shit. This isn't safe for you."

"I can't help it, Rye. He is my soulmate. I know it sounds stupid, but I need him. I need *us*. It's hard to explain, but he completes me."

"Okay, I'll go along with this... for now."

"Thank you. Come on, we have my husband's funeral to plan."

"You sound way happier about that than you should, Hol."

"He made me think he was dead for three bloody

days, Rye. I'm going to take pleasure in planning this funeral. It'll be therapeutic."

"Mrs. Valentino, are you sure about this? It's a lot."

"Father Thomas, my husband was a king. Are you saying that releasing a dove to symbolize each year he was on this earth is too much? I would think not."

"It's not just the doves, Mrs. Valentino. But an orchestra? Really? Theo didn't even like the symphony."

"Well, Theo's not here to decide what happens at his funeral. *I am.* And I like the symphony. What do you think, Gloria?" I ask her.

"I think my son would want you to have whatever you wanted, darling." She blots the corners of her eyes with a tissue.

"What I want is my husband back. Can you do that for me, Father Thomas? Tell your God that it's not his time. I don't want to be planning a funeral service. I don't want to be a bloody widow before I'm thirty. I want a lifetime of memories with my husband, not just a few weeks. I want to be the mother of his children. I want to grow old with him and watch our grandchildren run around. I want him back!" I yell. This whole planning a funeral thing is harder than I thought. It's surreal, even knowing that he's alive and this is all pretend. It hurts, like looking into what my future may hold. Rising to my feet, I push my chair into the table. "I'm sorry. I shouldn't have taken it out on you. Please just arrange a simple service. Quiet, family only." I walk out of the dining room and head for the garden.

I need to be alone. I need to clear my mind of the images of T's lifeless body lying in a coffin. I find a spot near the pond and sit on the ground. The air is chilly. I should have brought a coat... I pull the burner out of my pocket and read his message again and again—it feels like my only lifeline at the moment. The only connection I have to my husband.

Five minutes later, a silhouette blocks the sun and someone sits next to me. I keep my gaze straight ahead, staring at the water as I break the silence. "You knew, and you didn't tell me. You let me think the worst. You watched me fall apart. And still, nothing. Not a word."

"I'm sorry. I couldn't tell you. He shouldn't have told you either," Neo says.

"I hate you right now. I hate that you knew this entire time. And I hate him for doing this. I hate him for not being here."

"You don't hate him, Holly. You couldn't, even if you tried. We just have to get through this and then we can go back to normal."

"What will normal look like, Neo? How many funerals am I going to have to attend? To plan? This life that you guys live, it's not safe. I want him safe, and he's out there. Alone."

"Trust me, sweetheart, T's never alone. You might not see them, but there are always at least ten men surrounding him. Backing him up. Sometimes he doesn't even know they're there. He's my best friend, Holly. I'm not about to let anything happen to him."

"So, I guess we're just supposed to go along with this stupid plan? Fly to Sydney on Saturday and pretend that we're grieving?"

"Will you really be pretending? You saw him just last night, and yet you're out here, sulking like you haven't seen him in years."

"Shut up. I'm not sulking. I'm contemplating. It's different."

"Sure. So, are all the women in Australia as hot as you are? Because if so, I'm looking forward to this trip."

"There's at least one other woman who looks just like me, but she's married. Her husband may not be a badass mafia guy, but I wouldn't wanna be on his bad side either." I laugh.

"I know exactly who your brother-in-law is, Holly, and what he's capable of doing. Do you think I haven't done my research on everyone involved in your life? I'm good at my job, and it's my job to know shit."

"Really? So, I guess you know *everything* then, huh? Like how people in Australia carry Vegemite on them at all times to prevent a drop bear attack?"

"Funny, but I happen to have a case of the stuff

waiting for me at Helena's. Theo made her order it after that first night, when you walked in and joked about Vegemite toast."

"He did not. You're lying."

Neo shrugs. "Call her up and ask her yourself."

"No, I believe you. He probably would do something that stupid." I smile at the thought.

Chapter Nine

I'm watching the service from upstairs, hiding out in the church's attic. It's simple, not many words are said. But watching my mother and Holly suffer through this is too much. Holly knows it's not real, yet she looks as heartbroken as she did before learning the truth. Either she's a great actress, or this really is taking a fucking toll on her.

I have a jet ready to fly me to Italy, and as soon as I

know Holly is on her way back to Sydney, I'll be gone too. I was supposed to leave two days ago. I just couldn't go, knowing she'd be here alone.

I've ignored the messages and calls from the other three. They can all go fuck themselves. I don't trust a single fucking one of them. They wanted a ghost? Well, now they have one. I've spoken to Uncle Gabe, filled him in on what's happening. He's seated in the pew next to his son. Neo looks pissed off at the world, though that's not much different from how he usually looks. He's been giving me the cold shoulder the last two days. He's pissed that I pulled Holly further into this by telling her I was alive. I don't know what he expected me to do. I couldn't just sit back any longer and watch her break. At least now she knows I'm coming home. Nothing is going to stop me from fucking coming home to her.

The service concludes, and Holly stands with her sister and my mother. She looks up, almost like she's staring right at me. It's impossible for her to know that I'm here. But it's as if she can feel my presence none-theless. Her sister whispers something in her ear, and she nods before walking down the center aisle. I'm just about to slip out the back when the three fucking men I've been avoiding walk in and approach my wife. My teeth grind as I watch them greet her with their condo-lences. Motherfuckers. Thankfully, five of my guys interject and surround her—one going as far as to step *in front* of her.

Sonnie, I think his name is. I'll have to remember to give him a raise. He says something to the Dons, and they each respond with a similar glower. Neo and Uncle Gabe appear at her side, before leading her out of the church and into the waiting SUV. Confident that she's safe now, I jump into my beater car and follow them all the way to the airport. I watch her get out and climb the steps of the jet with her twin. Then I pull out my phone and send off a text.

Me: You look absolutely stunning today, dolcezza. Try to relax and have fun with your friends and family. Ti amo, sempre.

I glance back up at the jet, and Holly appears at the door with that same guard from inside the church. Again, he steps forward to shield her from view. Interesting... I feel like I've missed a lot being gone. She's either gained their respect, or Neo's put the fear of God into them. Holly scans the airfield, placing a palm to her forehead to block the sun, before her eyes land on my windshield. She pulls her phone out and types a message, my inbox pinging moments later.

Mine: I like your other car better, but if we had to disappear and live off the grid, I'd follow you anywhere in anything. Ti amo, sempre. Torna da me.

Come back to me. I read her message twice.

Always, dolcezza. Never doubt that.

I wait and watch Holly take off, before driving around to the hanger and boarding my own flight. Sitting down on the luxury upholstery, I close my eyes, only to open them when I feel someone occupy the seat next to me. I groan when I realize who it is. "What the fuck are you doing here?"

"You didn't think I'd let you go off on a suicide mission alone, did you?"

"It's not a fucking suicide mission. And I don't need *or want* you here."

"Too bad. We're here, and we're helping. It's partly my fault you got dragged into this mess in the first place. Well, not mine, but my family's anyway."

"It's solely your fucking family's fault, L. Do you have any idea what kind of shit your father and brother were into? Did you know?"

"I had my suspicions, but I didn't know for sure," she answers.

"Wait, *we*? You said *we're* here to help. Who else is on this fucking jet, L?"

"Ah, about that... Don't get mad, T. But he wouldn't let me come without him." I know who it is before she even says his name: the fucking Russian.

"Alexei promised to be on his best behavior. You'll barely notice he's here."

"You brought a fucking Russian on my jet, and you think I won't notice he's here?" I shake my head. "We're going to Italy, L. You're bringing a fucking Russian to Italy? I thought you were smarter than that."

"Well, I couldn't let you do this alone. And he wouldn't take no for an answer. Don't worry about Alexei. He can handle himself just fine, trust me." She shrugs. "So... I hear I have you to thank for blowing my brother to pieces."

I groan. I don't want to deal with this right now. "I have no idea what you're talking about, but I'm sure he won't be missed by anyone."

"You're right. He won't. Uncle Caleb is looking to take over. He'll get it cleaned up and restore the family name." Huh, I like her Uncle Caleb. We went to school together. He's the product of one of her grandfather's affairs. I'm surprised they're allowing an illegitimate son to run things. But it's not my place to tell another family how to handle their shit—not when it doesn't affect me and mine. "So, how's it feel to be dead? Your service was very plain for someone of your caliber. I would have thought your mother and wife would have put more effort into it," Lana muses.

"L, don't think I won't fucking kill you and throw you out the door over the fucking Atlantic Ocean.

Don't ever fucking speak disrespectfully about my wife again," I growl.

"Wait! I wasn't. I happen to like Holly very much —much more than I like your grumpy ass right now. I just thought it would be more of a send-off. Unless she knows."

"Shut up. I'm really not in the mood." The *fasten seat belt* sign dims, and I stand before making my way over to the bar and pouring myself a glass of whisky. "How'd you know I'd be here anyway?" I ask her.

"I have my ways. As soon as Alexei tried to get me to leave New York, I knew you were the only person who could have possibly wanted to warn me. Well, maybe Neo, but he seemed preoccupied with your widow."

"L, I swear to God, leave my wife out of any and all conversations, or it won't bode well for you."

"I'm not saying anything bad about her, Theo. You're wound too tight. I'm just glad I didn't end up in her shoes."

I laugh. "I never would have let that happen."

"You're welcome, by the way. You never did thank me for taking care of that problem."

"I'm not fucking thanking you for killing my father, Lana. Are you insane?"

She shrugs and looks down the walkway. "You can come out now," she calls as Alexei appears from behind the curtain.

"Great, there goes my fucking peaceful flight."

"Shut up and sit down. We have a plan to come up with."

Eight hours. Eight fucking hours, I had to sit and endure the torture of listening to Lana dictate what she thought should happen. Eight fucking hours, I was trapped on a jet with a Russian I wanted to strangle with my bare hands.

His only saving grace was that Lana seemed to really fucking like the idiot. I find myself, yet again, making concessions I wouldn't otherwise make for her. Despite how I feel about Lana right now, she was one of my best friends growing up. It was always Neo, Lana, and me—us against the world. I can't seem to let go of those years, of that bond we developed over underage partying. She used to confide in me about the boys she liked or dated.

When she lost her virginity in some jock's car, she came and told *me*. And I broke the fucker's knees, because she deserved better than to be fucked in the back seat like a goddamn streetwalker. Do I care about her? Yes. Do I fucking hate her for what she's done? Again, yes. I don't know how to fucking compartmentalize these feelings.

We've just landed in Italy, and I'm thankful for the

reprieve as we enter the small cottage I rented. I could go to the Valentino estate, but that would defeat the purpose of being dead. I don't want the other families to know of my whereabouts yet. The only positive thing that came from those eight hours on that fucking flight was the intel I managed to get out of Lana. I know every place her idiot brother frequented. One being a hole-in-the-wall strip club not far from here. I'm planning on walking down there later tonight, to see if I can find anything out about what ol' Johnny boy was up to and what he was looking to accomplish in New York.

I fire off a quick message to Holly. I don't want her to worry anymore, so I need to make a conscious effort to check in regularly.

Me: Just landed, safe and sound. Please let me know when you've touched down, dolcezza.

I know she's still in the air. The flight from New York to Sydney is over twice as long as the one to Rome.

Chapter Ten

Holly

"Can I just shoot him and put us all out of our misery already?" Neo whispers to me.

"Don't joke about that. You know he woke up from being in a coma not that long ago. *Because he was bloody shot*," I volley back.

"Okay, so no to the shooting." He holds his hands up in surrender.

I don't blame him. Bray's nonsense is even getting

on *my* last nerve. "Reilly, can't you distract him or something? You know there's a bedroom that way." I point to the back of the jet. I've been on private planes before. Bray's friend, Dean, has one. But this jet? This is like Trump-level money, I'm sure. I could live in this thing; it's that luxurious. The white leather seats are like sitting in a La-Z-Boy. They're so comfy.

"Fuck no! You think I'm going to let all the fucking men on this jet hear her scream when I make her come? Not a fucking chance!" Bray seethes.

"Well, man up and stop complaining."

"Holly, I love you. You're one of my favorite sisters-in-law. But if I die on this jet, I'm coming back to haunt your ass." Bray clings to the armrests.

"Tell me, Bray, who is your favorite? Me or Alyssa?" I ask him. Alyssa is one of my and Reilly's best friends; she's also married to Bray's older brother.

"That's not a question I'll ever answer," he says between clenched teeth.

"Well, obviously, it's me. It has to be."

"How do you figure?"

"Well, you love Reilly, and I'm literally her clone. So, technically, you love me too." I smile.

Neo laughs beside me. "Does that mean T will love your sister as much as he loves you, Hol?"

"What? No. T wouldn't..." *Shit, will Theo even be able to tell us apart?* I certainly hope he can.

"So, your theory is flawed," Bray counters.

"Shut up. When the plane goes down, I'm stealing

your oxygen mask." I poke my tongue out at him. Childish, I know.

"Don't worry, babe, I can take her. I'll get your mask back for you."

"I wouldn't be so sure... After all, your sister shot me in the chest a few weeks back, because she thought I was going to hurt her husband. She also held a gun to a Don's head, because he was in a fight with T. She's fiercer than anyone would ever expect." Neo smiles proudly at me.

"La nostra regina senza pretese," Sonnie offers quietly.

"Wait, what do you mean she shot you? She's afraid of guns." Reilly narrows her eyes.

"*Was* afraid of them. She actually fainted the first time she saw T pull a piece on me." Neo laughs.

"I didn't faint. I briefly lost consciousness. It's different," I argue.

"Hold up a second. Let's go back to you shooting someone, and what the fuck is this about you aiming a gun at a mob boss? You are joking, right?" Bray jumps to his feet and shouts in my direction. And within seconds, three men are standing in front of me—*a protective bunch, they are.*

I push my way through the wall of bodies. "Don't worry, his bark is way worse than his bite," I tell them, though they don't appear too impressed, nor do they back off. Interestingly enough, Neo is the only one who doesn't rise to my defense. "Aren't you—I don't know—

meant to protect me with your life or something?" I ask him, arching an eyebrow.

"And I absolutely fucking would, mia regina, if I thought you were actually in danger. Your brother-in-law is not a threat." Neo waves me off, going back to looking at his phone.

"Right, just checking." I turn to Bray, who is scrutinizing every word exchanged between me and my husband's second.

"What the fuck is going on, Holly? Are you in some kind of trouble?"

"No, I'm not." I fold my arms over my chest.

"Give her five minutes. I'm sure she'll manage to find some. She's like a fucking magnet for it," Neo mumbles.

"Not helping."

"Oh, I didn't know I was supposed to be helpful. Let me rectify that. Holly here caught the eye of my cousin, T. It was funny to watch. The guy fell fucking hard and fast. It was like the first coming of Jesus Christ himself—*a goddamn miracle*. I had lost all hope for T, and then Holly just happened to walk into my sister's coffee shop." Neo pauses for a breath. "At the time, my cousin was just the prince, the underboss, then his pops was taken out. Poisoned at the dinner table, terrible scene. May you rest in peace, Uncle." He stops to make the sign of the cross over his chest. "Anyway, with the passing of my uncle, T's old man and also the head of the Valentino family, my cousin was left the throne. And when he and young Holly here went and eloped, without telling a soul mind you, it made her our reigning queen."

"Fuck off, you did not go and marry into a crime family, Holly," Bray huffs.

"Let he who is without sin throw the first stone. Don't think I don't know all about your own misdeeds. And your brother's," Neo tosses back.

What's he saying? I knew the Williamsons weren't always on the up-and-up when it came to everything, but they're nothing like the Valentinos. I mean, they just ran a nightclub with a little illegal underground fighting. That's not that bad.

"I don't give a fuck what any of you fuckers do with your lives. However, I do give a fuck about how it's going to impact my wife... and my fucking sister-in-law," Bray growls.

I drop down into my seat. I don't want this lifestyle —*my choices*—to affect my sister. Or her husband. *I really don't.* I couldn't stand it if something were to happen to either of them. "I understand, if when we land, you no longer want anything to do with me," I say, looking at Bray and Reilly.

"What? Don't be stupid. Holly, you are my sister. I don't care what your last name is, or what your husband does or doesn't do for a living. Let's not forget that *he's* fucking dead, right? You're a widow, Hol. You don't have to stay around this broody lot if you don't want to."

"I'm sorry. I didn't mean to drag you guys into my mess. I think I need to lie down." I can't be here right now, not with everyone looking at me.

"Let me check the room first, Mrs. Valentino." Sonnie is quick to stand and walk down the hallway.

"What do you think is going to be in there, Sonnie? We are literally in the air. I don't think the boogeyman boarded mid-flight." I follow him.

"You can never be too careful, ma'am." And we're back to the *ma'am* thing. "All clear," he announces, walking out and holding the door open.

"Mmm, you don't say." I smile at him. "Thank you for being so cautious." I close the door, lie down on the bed, pull the phone out of my pocket, and open the message thread from T. There are only a couple, but reading them gives me some sort of reassurance. I want him back so badly. Knowing he's alive and out there doing God knows what... it's terrifying.

But at least I know he's alive. That alone gives me comfort. Then again, would I even know if something were to happen to him? How would I find out? Surely Neo would tell me.

I must have drifted off at some point, because when I open my eyes again, it's to Reilly shaking me. "Hol, wake up. We're about to land. Come on, you need to sit back down and buckle up."

"Just five more minutes," I say.

"Nope, get up. No more time." She throws the covers off me. "Um, Holly, why do you have the world's most-outdated phone?"

Her question has me bolting upright. "Shh. It's a burner. T left it for me. It's the only way I have to get a hold of him."

"You've been in contact with him?"

"Yes, he's been texting." I open the message thread and show her.

"Okay then, but are you sure this guy is really for you, Hol?"

"I love him, Rye. Do you think I'm crazy to want him?"

"I don't think you're crazy. I think you're in love." She tries to hug me.

Hold that thought. I know T said to only contact him for emergencies. But my sister needing to see for herself why my husband's *worth it* counts, right? I mean, if she hears him, how we just *work* together, she'll get it. She has to. I press call on the only name in the phone. He answers on the second ring. "Dolcezza, what's wrong?" Shit, he sounds panicked. I shouldn't have called. It's not an emergency...

"I'm okay. I just... I miss you." I sigh. Hearing his voice doesn't make me miss him any less. It fucking hurts how much I want him near me.

"I fucking miss you too. Dolcezza, are you sure you're okay? Have you landed in Sydney yet?"

"No, we are circling now. We should be landing soon. Are you okay?" I ask.

"Apart from not being able to reach out and hold you, I'm okay."

"I don't like this."

"I don't either. Torno da te appena posso. I swear it won't be for long, Holly. When I get to Sydney, this will all be a distant memory."

"I'm sorry for calling. I know I shouldn't," I tell him, though I don't mean it, because I at least got to hear his voice.

"Don't be sorry. Talking to you is like a balm for my aching soul, dolcezza."

"Are you sure you don't want to quit the family gig and go to Hallmark?" I laugh.

"It's tempting. But no. I have to go, Holly. I love you. Remember: torno da te appena posso."

"I remember. Make sure you do. Wait, that does mean you're coming back to me as soon as you can, right?"

I hear his chuckle through the receiver. "Yes, you're picking up on the language rather quickly, dolcezza."

"Well, I'm determined to know what everyone around me is saying. I might sign up for Italian lessons in Sydney. It could be a fun way to kill some time while I wait. Also, you never know. With my luck, I could get some hot, young Italian stallion as my tutor."

"Holly, don't think my reach is limited because I'm 10,000 miles away. Believe me when I say this: any motherfucker even trying to get too close to you will find themselves at the bottom of the Pacific."

"Well, you should hurry up and get back to me, because I'm starving and my new favorite flavor is Italian."

"Great, now I'm walking down the fucking street with a hard-on. Thanks, dolcezza."

"You're welcome. I love you, T. Be safe."

"Always. I love you too. Don't do anything reckless, and make sure you stick with security or at the very least Neo."

"Okay." I hang up and stare at the phone.

"Oh my God, even his voice is hot, Holly. No wonder you're smitten. Okay, so you guys really do love each other—*thank God*. But we still have to pretend he's dead, right?"

"Yeah. Why?"

"Because you're a young, heartbroken widow, who married a billionaire. I mean, I'm assuming from his closet and this jet that he's loaded. So... we, sister, are going to burn a hole in that man's credit card. We're going shopping," she squeals.

"I'm not sure how shopping is meant to help me grieve."

"It won't. It's a distraction. Come on, we need to go

and buckle up so we can land." I slip the burner into my pocket and follow Reilly back into the cabin. Everyone is waiting on us. "Sorry, she's a pain in the ass to wake up," she offers, taking the seat closest to Bray.

I sit next to Neo, who is still typing shit on his phone. "Did you leave a special lady behind?" I probe.

"Nope." He answers by tucking the device into his jacket.

"Okay. Ah, when we land, what are we doing with everyone? I could get away with taking you to my parents' house but not the rest of them." I really didn't think this out.

"You can't stay at your parents' place, Holly. It's not secure enough. Don't worry, Theo bought a compound in the city, the day after he met you. I thought he was crazy at the time, but I guess it's coming in handy now."

"He bought a compound? Like a house? In Sydney? Why?"

"Because he's a lovesick fool with way too much money to burn."

"Huh. When you say *too much* money... T gave me these cards with my name on them, but I haven't used them yet. Any idea what their limits are, or how I find out?"

Neo looks at me like I've lost my mind. "Are the cards black?"

"Yes."

"There is no limit, Holly."

"What do you mean there's no limit? Everything has a limit."

"Have you really not checked out your husband's finances? I know for a fact he put your name down on all the accounts. You have access to everything."

I shrug. "I've never thought about it before. I don't need his money, Neo."

Chapter Eleven

I'm on cloud nine after speaking to Holly. This not being able to hold her, to kiss her whenever I want, it's getting old. I'm like a fucking junkie, going through withdrawals and scrambling for any tiny crumb I can get. And at the moment, those tiny crumbs consist of a text message or a short phone call. It's fucked up. Just when I found her, we're pulled apart by external forces. I need to focus. Because I know at the end of this job, I'll be going home to my wife.

I'm heading into that seedy strip club—the one John Junior was known to patronize. I don't understand why someone with so much wealth at their disposal would come to a place like this. He could afford high-class hookers if that was what he was into. I show my fake ID to the bouncer, and he lets me pass without even glancing at it. Either I look fucking old, or they just don't care.

I probably look like I'm fucking fifty with the bags under my eyes. I haven't been sleeping. I've been lucky to catch a good three hours a night. Without my wife next to me, I can't fucking settle. Before Holly, I'd never slept next to a woman. And now I fucking need that woman to be able to sleep. Whatever hold she has on me, it runs fucking deep. And I'm not about to cut that cord.

I head for the bar and order a whisky—in English. I'll let everyone think I'm a tourist, visiting the birthplace of his ancestors. The patrons will be more loose-lipped around me if they think I can't speak the language. I may have been born in the US, but make no mistake, my family's legacy still ties back to Sicily. The Valentino family is well known in the homeland. My uncle is currently a Don there. I could tell him I'm close by, and I'd have everything at my disposal.

As much as I trust my family, there is always that little bit of doubt in the back of my mind. I find it hard to believe that the Sicilian connections didn't know what John Junior was into with that Irish fucker. I just don't understand why they haven't put a stop to it yet. It concerns their daughters, their sisters, their grand-daughters, their cousins—all being kidnapped off the street and sold. Those girls I saw were natives, either to the islands or the mainland. Their pleas were uttered in fluent Italian.

I wonder if the team I sent into that warehouse got them out. I need to check in with Neo to determine the fallout... The other three wanted me to forget those girls and move on to the bigger fish here. The problem was: *I couldn't forget.* I hope my cousin got to them before the auction took place.

After thirty minutes of sitting at this rundown bar, two overweight slobs—in suits that hang off their shoul-ders—sit down next to me. One of them turns and grunts, "Come va?" *How are you?*

I screw my face up in confusion before calling out to the bartender. "Another one."

The newcomers scrutinize me for a moment before turning back around and going about their conversa-tion. I pull out my phone and hold it to my ear. "Babe, I'll be back soon. I'm just picking up some food," I say and hang up. The men next to me chuckle and make a comment about Americans.

I listen in on their exchange as best I can with the music blaring. I feign disinterest and scroll through my phone. I'm looking at photos of Holly, pictures I took when she wasn't watching. Ones of her working in my office and ones of her sleeping. I love capturing her likeness in those moments when she's not aware I'm observing her. These images are pure, raw, and fucking gorgeous.

"John Junior è fuori. Ho sentito che il trifoglio arriverà in città la prossima settimana." One of the men next to me whispers to his friend. *John Junior is out* —yeah, because I fucking took him out, motherfucker. But the part about *the Clover coming to town*—now, that's interesting.

I order another drink, swirling the liquid around in my cup before throwing it back.

"You know, Donatello is getting suspicious. He knows something is going on. Heads will roll when he figures it out, and I for one won't be on the wrong fucking team when that happens," the other guy responds. Donatello... maybe I should inform him of my presence. Then again, he probably already fucking knows. This is his country after all; he should know who's coming and going. "Pensi che andranno fino in fondo? Prendere la nipote di Donatello è un vaffanculo."

My hand clenches around my glass. They're talking about taking Donatello's granddaughter. What fucking idiota is stupid enough to try something like that? My mind is running through the possibilities. Does he know about their plans? Is that why *they* wanted me here? How deep does this go? I've been in the country less than a day, and I've managed to stumble across this information fairly easily. Surely a man of Donatello's standing would be aware of the threat already... unless his rat is high up in the ranks.

"He won't see it coming. He'd never suspect his underboss to be cutting him out. Giovani knows the way to send the old man spiraling is by making his precious princess disappear." Giovani? I type the name into my phone. I know who the fucker is. Is he really capable of betraying Donatello though? Anything's possible. This is the reason I never fully trust anyone; someone is always looking to outdo you. Holly may be the only exception to that rule. That woman would have my back no matter what. I know it. She's proven it time and time again. I stand on wobbly legs and fall into the guy beside me. "Watch it!" he yells in broken English.

"Sorry, bud, shouldn't have had that last one," I slur and make my way to the door. It's not until I'm in the shadows of the sidewalk and on my way back to the shitty little condo, that I take out the phone I swiped from the fat fucker at the bar.

"Get a fucking room. Jesus Christ!" I curse as I enter the condo to find Lana and Alexei on the sofa. Naked. Naked on the goddamn sofa. Fucking! Some things you cannot unsee. Alexei's white fucking Russian ass being one of them.

"Shut up. You're just jealous you're not getting any. What did you find out?" Lana's footsteps follow me into the kitchen. I don't turn around. "Please tell me you at least put fucking clothes on before walking in here."

"Of course she has clothes on. You think I'd let your depraved ass see her naked," Alexei growls.

Spinning around, I smirk at him. "What makes you think I haven't already? We were engaged for two years, you know." I haven't, and I don't ever fucking want to, but he doesn't need to know that. Seconds later, I'm looking down the barrel of a Glock.

"Fuck you. You dirty fucking Italian bastard," Alexei grunts. The smirk doesn't drop from my face, and not because I think he isn't capable of pulling the trigger. I know he is. No, it's because I know he *won't*— Lana would never allow him to take me out.

"L, be a doll and rein in your boyfriend," I tell her before turning back around and stalking away. "Also, a word of advice, *comrade*: You're in Italy. If you plan on making it out alive, try to refrain from ever repeating that phrase." I head to my room and grab my phone. I know I spoke to Holly not that long ago, but I need to hear her voice.

"T, are you okay?" She sounds rushed, breathless, when she finally picks up.

"Holly, what's wrong? Why are you panting?" I

ask, already pulling up Neo's number on my spare burner.

"I was in the shower. I ran out when I heard the phone ringing," she says.

"You were in the shower? So, right now, you're naked? Dripping wet and naked for me?"

"I have a towel on. But, yes, other than that, I'm dripping wet everywhere else."

"Where are you?"

"At the *way-over-the-top* house you bought in Bondi. Are we moving to Sydney? Why would you buy such a big property here, T?"

"I bought it for us. We'll grow into it. We're not moving, Holly, but we'll vacation there a lot, I suspect."

"Oh, okay."

"Are you in the master suite?"

"Yes."

"Go lock the door," I instruct her. I hear her footsteps and then a click.

"Holly, you need to learn to lock your doors. You were in the shower. Anyone could have walked in."

"Well, the last time someone just so happened to help themselves into my space, I ended up marrying the guy, so I'd say that tends to work out well for me." She laughs.

"Your safety is not a joke. Now, go and lie on the bed."

"Oh, bossy much? Why am I lying on the bed? I'm going to get water all over the blankets."

"I'll buy you new blankets. Just do it."

"Okay, I'm on the bed," she says.

"Undo the towel, dolcezza. Run your hands over your breasts." I close my eyes, the image of her following my instructions as vivid as if I were seeing it firsthand.

"Wait, no. I can't do this, T. I mean, I've-I've never done this sort of thing before. Hold on, you're trying to have phone sex with me, aren't you? Oh my God, just end me now." She's rambling. Even her ramblings turn me the fuck on.

"Holly, relax. You can do this. Have you never masturbated before?" I ask her, knowing full well she has. I've seen the contents of her bedside drawers.

"Well, of course I have, but that's different. That's by myself. I've never had an audience."

"You don't have an audience, dolcezza. It's just you and me. Close your eyes and listen to my voice. Let me make you feel good."

"Okay. But just so you know, if I get like gun-shy or something, I still had a good time."

I can't help but laugh. She's thanking me before we've even started. "Holly, close your eyes, then take your right hand and circle your fingers around your breast... *lightly*."

"Okay."

"Pinch your nipple between your fingers for me, dolcezza."

"Mmhmm." She lets out a little moan.

"I want you to imagine that they're my hands on you. Reach down further. Run your fingertips up the smooth skin of your inner thigh. Fuck, I want to feel your skin so badly right now. I want to bury my head between those thighs and feast for days."

"I want that. All of that. I want it too."

"I want you to slowly swipe your index finger up the center of your slit."

"Oh, God," she moans.

"Tell me... are you wet for me, Holly? Dip your finger inside your tight pussy and tell me how wet you are."

"Oh, God. Ah, mmhmm," she mumbles.

"Tell me, dolcezza," I command.

"Yes, I'm wet, so damn wet."

I chuckle. "Good girl. I knew you would be. How much do you want my fingers on you, *in you*, right now? How much do you want my tongue licking up your juices, dolcezza? Do you want my cock filling you to the brim, thrusting in and out, until you fall apart?" I take my cock in my hand, and precum leaks from the tip.

"I want all of it, T. Damn it, I'm so bloody turned on." Her voice is husky, her need evident.

"I'm stroking my cock for you, dolcezza. It's rock-hard and all yours. I want you to circle your fingers around your clit, slowly."

"Mmm, T, I need to—"

"Don't you dare come yet, Holly. We come together. *Wait.* Put two fingers in that pussy of mine."

"T, I need to... I can't... Oh, God."

"I'm so close. Hearing you get yourself off for me is fucking hot, Holly. Tell me what you need?"

"I need you, damn it. I need you so bloody bad," she cries out.

"Holly, I want you to come now! Come for me. Let go and take yourself over that edge, dolcezza. Fuck!" I growl as I spill my own cum all over my stomach.

"Yes! Holy hell," she whispers before everything goes silent—the only sound coming from the other end of the line is her heavy breathing.

"Fuck, I love you."

"Right back at ya. Gosh, if I knew phone sex could be like that, I would have tried it a whole lot sooner." I can hear the smile in her tone.

"I'm not biting, Holly. I like being your first at things. How about next time we step it up to video?" My cock hardens again at the thought.

"Mmm, maybe I'll hold out until I get to have you in person. You know, give you some incentive to hurry up and come home."

"I have plenty of incentive to come home. You are all the incentive I need." Fuck, I've never missed anyone as much as I fucking miss this woman. I miss everything about her. Her smell, her touch, her voice, her laughter. I miss seeing her mass of red hair spilled out on the pillows as she sleeps. "I fucking miss you so damn much, dolcezza. I love you."

"I love you too. I didn't think it was possible to miss someone this much. But it's easier knowing that you're coming back. When I thought you were..." She stops mid-sentence.

"I know. I'm sorry for doing that to you. I will never do that to you again. But you have to promise me something."

"What?"

"If anything were to happen... I don't want you to suffer. Promise me you'll find a way to move on and be happy again, that you'll never hurt yourself no matter how much it hurts in the moment." I can't stop seeing her on the floor with that piece of glass in her hands... envisioning the thoughts that were going through her head. If Neo hadn't gotten into that room, would she have done it? Would she have sliced into her wrist?

"I can't promise that. I want to, but I don't want a life that doesn't include you, Theo. Just hurry up and come back to me."

Fuck! She fucking hung up. I really wanted that promise.

Chapter Twelve

Holly

I throw the phone across the bed. Fuck him! Who does he think he is, trying to get me to make such a stupid promise? My phone starts ringing immediately. I ignore it, and the ringing stops only to be followed by the beeps of an incoming text. Again, I ignore it, get up, and look for clothes. I dig through my suitcase for something comfortable. I find a pair of denim cutoffs and a black tank top. Those will work.

Then I throw on a pair of Converse; I'm going to need sensible footwear for all the walking I plan to do today.

The phone has continued to beep on the bed as I get dressed. I pick up and read through the messages, all from Theo. No surprise there, considering he's the only one who knows the number. He's probably never had a girl hang up on him before.

Yours: Holly, did you seriously hang up on me?

Yours: Answer your phone, Holly…

Yours: Holly, call me.

Yours: Those are way too fucking short. You are not wearing that out of the room.

The last one has me pausing. I look around. Of course that fucker has cameras hooked up in here. I text him back.

Me: Have the cameras removed from the room, Theo, or I'm going to stay at my parents' house.

I dig out my actual phone from my bag and send a group text to the girls: Reilly, Alyssa, and our other friend, Sarah.

Me: We're going shopping today. I have multiple unlimited cards to burn through!

Their replies filter in almost instantly.

Reilly: YES! Pick me up. I'm so ready for this. Also, when are you telling the girls about your husband?

Sarah: Husband? WTF! What did I miss, Holly? Also, I can't. I'm working today. Sorry!

Alyssa: Holly, details, I need them now! Count me in! I need to escape my over-bearing hubby for a few hours anyway.

I smile. I knew I could count on these girls. This is so out of my element. I've never been much of a shopper. My sister is a different story, and she has great taste. It's time Holly 2.0 got a new look. I send them back a message, while the burner phone is constantly ringing in my other hand.

Me: I'll fill you in when I see you both. Rye, be there in thirty. Then I'll come get you, Lyssa.

I tuck my phone into my bag, look up, and smile. I don't know where the cameras are hidden, but I know he's watching me. I slam the door and only make it five steps down the hallway before Neo is in front of me, holding his phone out. "Your husband is insisting on talking to you," he says.

"Tell my husband that I'm currently *otherwise occupied*. I'm heading out." I go to slip past him, but he stops me.

"Hold up. Where are you going? And it sure as hell isn't anywhere by yourself. Let me get the keys." Neo presses the mute button on his phone and stares me directly in the eyes. "Look, I don't know what the idiot did to piss you off, but you need to speak with him, Holly. He's over in Italy. Do you really want to carry the burden of regret... if something were to go wrong?"

"What's going to go wrong? Is he in trouble?" I start to panic. Neo is right. I'm being childish. I shouldn't ever reject Theo's calls. I pull the phone out of his hand and unmute it. "I want the cameras removed."

"And I want you to go back into that bedroom and put something more appropriate on—something that actually covers your ass cheeks, Holly," he growls.

I roll my eyes, running my palms down the back of my shorts. "My ass is covered just fine. I'm sorry for hanging up on you, but you pissed me off. Now, if you don't need anything, I'm going shopping with my sister."

"I love you, Holly. I want you to be safe and happy. *Always*. I need to know that you'll be okay... always," he says quietly.

"There is no way I will ever be okay without you. I'm not making you promises I can't keep. I love you too, by the way. Even if I am really bloody mad at you right now."

"Okay, go enjoy the day with your sister, *after* you change your outfit," he adds.

"Bye, T." I hang up and hand the phone back to Neo, who is staring at me, wide-mouthed.

"What?" I ask, feeling a sense of self-consciousness creep in.

"You just hung up on him," he states.

"It wasn't the first time, and it probably won't be the last. Reilly is expecting me. I really do need to go."

"Okay, let's go." Neo holds his arm out for me to walk past.

"It's Sydney, Neo. Nothing is going to happen to me here. I don't need you following me around all day."

He ignores me and calls out through the house. "Sonnie, you're with us."

And the next thing I know, I'm in the back of a black SUV with Neo in the passenger seat and Sonnie at the wheel. "Where to, Mrs. Valentino?" Sonnie asks.

"It's Holly, Sonnie. Call me Holly. We're going to Reilly's first. I'm sure the all-knowing man beside you can tell you where she lives." I smirk. But the smile dies on my face when Neo does in fact punch Reilly's address into the navigation system.

"I can't wait to see Zac flip his lid," Reilly says as the car pulls to a stop at the curb of Alyssa and Zac's building.

She goes to open the door. "Don't. You need to wait for one of us to make sure everything is clear first," Sonnie says, pressing the lock function.

"Ah, no, I don't. Open the fucking door, you buffoon!" Reilly yells.

"Rye, it's okay. Just let Neo get the door." I've gotten used to this routine, although I have no idea what kind of danger they think we could possibly be in here.

"You're always too agreeable, Holly," she groans.

"Yeah, well, I wasn't very agreeable when I hung up on my husband this morning. Oh, he also demanded that I change out of these shorts before I left the house." I smirk, knowing that's one way to get my sister's feathers ruffled.

"He *what*? How did he even know what you were wearing?" she asks, confused.

"Cameras. They're freaking everywhere in that house."

"You can always come and stay with me," she offers sincerely, with worry etched on her face.

"No, she can't," Sonnie replies. "The compound is the most secure place for Mrs. Valentino."

Reilly looks at me, slack-jawed. "Is this guy for real?" she questions.

"Yep." I pop the P right as Neo opens the door.

"Great, finally. What took so long? Couldn't quite figure out how doors work?" Reilly glares at him.

"You know, most people wouldn't dare speak to me like that. I'd have their tongues removed before they even finished their sentence," Neo states calmly.

"Yeah, well, I'm not most people. I'm the sister." Reilly walks off ahead of us and into the building.

I take a deep breath, waiting for the shitshow that is Zac Williamson and his bossy, brooding, overbearing self—which will kick in when we try to take Alyssa out. I hear it as soon as the doors of the lift open into their penthouse. "No, absolutely not, sunshine. You're eight months pregnant. You should be here. At home. Resting. With me."

"I'm going shopping with the girls, whether you like it or not, Zac. Get over it. I'll be fine. Women have been having babies since the beginning of time!" Alyssa yells at him.

"Not *my* woman. Not you. Sunshine, if you want to go shopping, I'll take you," he counters.

"Sorry, bro, girls' trip. You're not invited." Reilly laughs.

Zac pivots on his heel, sending Reilly a glare to envy all glares. "*You*, stay out of it." Then he turns, his scrutinizing gaze running over me. "Holly, you look... good?" It comes out as a question. I know I dressed differently than I normally would. But it's hot, and I was pissed off at my husband.

"Thanks. We won't keep her out all day, Zac. We're just doing a little shopping," I say in the sweetest voice I can manage. But he ignores me, and instead focuses over my shoulder. I look behind me to see Neo standing there with an equally penetrating gaze.

Though, it does nothing to sway Zac. No, the guy

has no sense of self-preservation. "Holly, a friend of yours, I take it?" he questions.

"Uh-huh, Zac, Neo. Neo, Zac." I motion between them, to which Zac raises an eyebrow at me. "He's my husband's cousin," I add. How else am I meant to introduce Neo to people? I can't exactly say: *Hey, this is Neo, the underboss of the Valentino crime family. Oh! And he's also my husband's cousin... my husband, you know, the Don.*

Zac is way too observant for his own good. He knows something is off with me. "And why is your husband's cousin standing in my apartment?" he prompts.

I don't really know how to explain that one. I look to Neo, and he steps closer to me. "I'm just the driver. Nice to meet you." He holds his hand out. He's a quick thinker.

Zac accepts the gesture and offers a palm. "Did you lose your license in the few weeks you were in New York?"

"She probably should. Have any of you seen this one drive?" Neo laughs.

"Unfortunately, many times," Reilly groans at the mention of the subject.

"So, where is this husband I've heard nothing about?" Zac questions.

"He died," Neo answers for me. I scowl at him. I know I'm not meant to tell anyone, but these are my friends, *my family.* I can trust them. I know I can.

Besides, I'm proud to be T's wife. I want to shout it from the tallest skyscraper in Sydney.

"We are *pretending* he died. Long story. Don't really have time to tell it. But he's working, in Italy. He'll be here in a couple of weeks." My words come out fast. I'm really not good at this. I hate lying— although, *technically*, I'm not. Theo *is* working in Italy.

"What does he do?" And that's the question I'm not prepared for. And of course Zac would be the one to ask it.

"He, ah, he…"

"Runs the family businesses. Busy man, that one." Neo jumps to my rescue again.

"Okay, well, I'd love to stay and chitchat, but I've got shops to hit. Let's go." Reilly starts towards the door.

"You two go ahead. Alyssa and I will be there in a minute." Zac takes his wife's hand, leaning in as he whispers something in her ear. I watch as she nods her head in agreement.

"I'll meet you there. I just need to use the bathroom first. This baby won't get off my bladder." She smiles at us.

"Okay." I follow Reilly into the lift. I'm not sure what to think about that exchange. Is this going to happen every time I try to hang out with my friends? Being forced to have an entourage that'll make people uncomfortable? Halfway through our descent, Neo presses the emergency button on the lift.

"What's wrong?" he asks me with genuine concern.

"Nothing. You know you're not meant to press that button unless it's an actual emergency?"

He smirks. "Far from the worst crime I've committed, bella. Now, cut the bullshit and tell me what's wrong?"

"Holly, what's wrong?" Reilly parrots.

"Nothing is wrong. I don't know. Is that normal? Is that how people are going to act towards me now? Not want to hang around me?"

"What? No. Trust me, Hol, you're going to have more assholes trying to hang around you *because of* who you are. I'm sure your friend's husband just wants to drive her himself. He came off a little controlling like that." Neo shrugs. "Besides, if your friends don't want to go shopping with you, you'll always have me. I happen to love shopping, and I have a great sense of style." He presses the button, and the lift settles into motion again.

I smile at him. He's probably right. Zac *is* controlling. And looking at Neo, dressed in what Reilly has already informed me (more than once this morning) is a Tom Ford suit, I can appreciate his fashion choices.

Chapter Thirteen

Holly

The morning started off with me wanting to blow my way through these fancy black cards. I've yet to even swipe one thing on them though. I've purchased plenty of new clothes (all of which Reilly tells me are perfect), while the groans and straight-out *NOs* I've been getting from Neo (as soon as I come out of the dressing rooms) tell me that the outfit is most definitely a *yes*. If he doesn't like them, then Theo most definitely won't approve either. Maybe next time he'll think twice before commenting on what I wear.

We've just sat down for lunch. I was surprised that Alyssa did meet us at the store, with Zac hot on her heels. Although, sitting in the middle of the food court, eating greasy hamburgers and fries with Neo and Zac, is a little unsettling. They both seem to be on high alert, their eyes constantly scanning their surroundings. Sonnie refused to sit down. He's standing with his back to me and his arms crossed while staring out into the crowd. People are looking at him, probably wondering who we are and why we are important enough to have our own security.

"Neo, make him sit down. It looks weird," I whisper.

"He's doing his job, Holly. A job he can't do if he's sitting down getting too comfortable.

"And what is his job?" Zac interjects.

"He's security. His job is to ensure nobody gets within two feet of this one, our little regina." Neo points a finger in my direction.

"Huh, queen? Hey, did you go and marry a king, Hol?" Zac cocks a brow. He knows. He's messing with me right now and hoping to make me squirm. How the hell does he know? Bloody Bray.

"Shut up, Zac. I know you know exactly what and who Theo is. We are not discussing this here. Actually, we are not discussing my husband *at all* when he's not around. You're more than welcome to discuss all of his affairs with him, *directly,* after he arrives. Want me to schedule you in for a meeting?" I'm getting worked up. I can't help how defensive I am when it comes to that man. Everyone at the table is staring at me with wide eyes. I've never been this outspoken person. I don't know where it's coming from. I can feel my face heating up, my skin turning red.

"Yeah, T is a touchy subject for this one. She actually shot me straight in the chest, because we were brawlin'." Neo laughs.

Zac's eyebrows jump up, but he shakes his head at Neo, like he doesn't believe him. "I don't need a meeting with your husband, Holly. I just need to make sure that my family doesn't get caught in the crossfire. And that includes you—*you* are part of my family too."

"Thank you. But, as you can see, I'm constantly surrounded by overbearing, overprotective men, who think they need to shield me from a threat that clearly doesn't exist here." I wave my hand from Neo to Sonnie.

Zac shrugs. "You can never be too careful, Hol. It'd be wise of you to listen to them."

"Oh, shit! Incoming, two o'clock. Holly, don't look," Reilly hisses.

Of course I can't help but crane my neck. And, yep, I regret it the moment I do. Heading straight towards us, *towards me,* is none other than Brett. A sleazy car salesman I went on a whole three dates with. All double dates with Reilly before she met Bray.

Sonnie steps straight in front of me, blocking my view. Neo is on his feet and around the table within seconds of seeing Brett beeline in our direction. I watch as Neo's hand reaches behind him and into his waistband. He's going to... Oh shit.

"Neo, no!" I jump up and walk around them. I may not want to talk to (or deal with) the kind of guy who only makes eye contact with my chest, but I also don't need Neo going all mafia badass on a relatively harmless sleazeball.

"Holly, I thought that was you. Babe, it's been way too long," Brett says, ignoring the two men at my back. He goes to wrap his arms around me, but I'm pulled away before he's within reach.

I gasp at the shock of being lifted and placed right next to Sonnie. "Hands off. You're not to touch her. And if your eyes don't shoot upwards and start looking at her in a more respectful manner, I will gladly rip them straight out of their sockets." Sonnie smirks. "It's a lot easier than it sounds," he adds.

Brett's gaze immediately rises to my face, and he glares between me and my burly bodyguard. He shakes his head. "I'll, uh, see you around, Holly." He makes a quick escape, walking away as fast as he can without flat-out running.

"Was that really necessary?" I turn to Sonnie.

"He was going to touch you, ma'am. I have strict orders that *no one is to touch you*."

"Yeah, I bet you do." I'm not really mad about the encounter. I didn't actually want sleazy Brett to hug me, but I would also like to be able to handle things myself. I could have managed him without their help. "I have a stop to make, then we can head home," I say to Reilly and Alyssa.

"You know, if you want to get even with T for whatever shit he did to piss you off this morning, this is the kind of place where you actually swipe one of those black cards," Neo whispers as he stands right beside me.

We are in the middle of a lingerie store. It's unsettling having him in here with me. "Can you like just wait outside or something? And why would me buying underwear get even with T?"

"Because he'll see the transaction. He'll look up the store. And then he'll be stuck wondering what you bought while he's desperate to see you in it. Trust me, it'll drive him nuts. I'll wait right at the doors." Neo walks to the entrance, where he and Sonnie position themselves like two statues. Zac is busy somewhere else in the store, picking up things and telling Alyssa she needs them, to which she rolls her eyes and puts everything back on the shelf.

I grab a few sets and find Reilly. "I need your help. Come with me." I drag her into the dressing room and hand her the crappy burner phone. "I need pictures, ones that will make me look hot." I blush.

"My-my, Hol, are you planning on sending naughty pictures to the mysterious husband?"

"Yes, I want him to suffer, Rye. Make sure these pictures will, you know..." I can't even say it. It's strange... When I'm talking to T, I feel like I can say anything. But with my own sister, I can't finish the sentence.

"You want him to have blue balls. Got it..." Reilly directs me, and I pose while she snaps away. "Okay, these should do the trick." Handing me the phone back, she says, "Give him hell, sis. I'll be outside."

"Wait, I'm not sending them now. I'll send them later. He's probably asleep anyway."

"The twenty or so unread messages from a contact named *Yours* would suggest otherwise." She smirks as she walks out of the changing room. I sit down on the bench and open the messages. I scroll past the first few and head to the last four.

Yours: Neo tells me you're not using your credit cards. Use them. I don't want you spending your own money, Holly.

Yours: The money in OUR accounts is yours too. Use it.

Yours: I really fucking hate that you're ignoring me, dolcezza.

Yours: Holly, I love you. I'm sorry if I said something to upset you, but you need to fucking talk to me. Please.

Okay, now I'm starting to feel bad. I shouldn't be ignoring him. Neo was right this morning. If anything were to happen to Theo in Italy, I'd never forgive myself, especially if we weren't on speaking terms. I start to text him back but decide to call instead. He must be sitting on the phone, because it barely rings once before he answers. "Holly, are you okay?" The concern in his voice is clear.

"Apart from being the biggest bitch on the planet, I'm okay. I'm sorry. I shouldn't have ignored you. It was childish and stupid." I swipe at the tear running down my cheek.

T sighs into the receiver. "Dolcezza, you are not even close to being a bitch. You are the sweetest, most considerate, caring person I've ever met. I was an ass and selfish. And I'm sorry."

"I love you, Theo, and I hate that you're not here. I'm literally sitting in a dressing room at Honey Bird-ette, crying, because all I want to do is lie in bed. *With you.*"

"What's Honey Birdette? And where are Neo and Sonnie?"

"They're both waiting at the store entrance," I say.

"Why the fuck aren't they with you? They're supposed to be no more than two feet away, Holly. Let me call Neo." He curses.

"Ah, T, wait... I told them to stay at the entrance. I mean, if you really want your cousin helping me try on underwear, then by all means, send him in."

"What? You're trying on underwear?" he repeats.

"It's a lingerie store."

"Hold on a sec." The line cuts out. I'm about to call him back when a video request pops up on the screen.

I press accept, and those dark eyes greet me along with that panty-melting smile. "Your face is danger-ously pretty," I blurt out.

Theo chuckles. "Not sure I've ever been called *pretty* before, dolcezza."

I lift a shoulder in response while wiping the remnants of tears off my face. My eyes are red and puffy. I look like shit.

"Please don't cry. I can't stand it when you cry, especially when I'm not there to hold you."

"I'm sorry. I'm okay. I just really, really miss you."

"I know." There's silence for a minute as we just stare at each other. Then a familiar glint flashes over T's eyes. "Holly, hold the phone out. What are you wearing?" he says.

I turn the camera, so it faces the mirror in front of me, and stand to give T a full-body view. I'm wearing a matching black leather and lace set. It's like something out of a bondage magazine, with straps that wrap around my breasts and twist up my neck, while the panties have three thick black bands and gold buckles at the sides.

"Fuck, holy shit. Yes, you're buying that." He breathes in.

"Maybe." I shrug.

"Holly, sit back down on the bench."

Chapter Fourteen

I t's killing me that Holly is on the other side of the world right now. *Wearing that.* I want to tear it off her body with my goddamn teeth. I watch as she sits back down on the bench. Before I instruct her further, I send Neo a text.

Me: Make sure no one gets near those dressing rooms for the next fifteen minutes. At least.

Neo: Seriously, T? We're in the middle of a fucking shopping center. What the fuck are you going to do in that room when you're all the way in Italy?

Me: You don't need to know. Just make sure no one can see or hear her.

Then I focus back on my wife—my hot-as-sin, fuck-able wife. "Holly, spread your legs." I wait for her to do as she's told. She looks around the room, unsure, but she complies. "Good girl. Now spread 'em wider for me."

"Ah, T, I'm in a bloody changing room. This is going to have to wait. I'm not doing this here."

"Yes, you are. I want you to pull those panties off. They're blocking my view of heaven."

"Argh, God. I'm only taking them off, because if I don't, I'll be at risk of ruining them. How am I meant to hand over wet panties at the counter, T?" She rambles on as she pulls the material down, kicks it to the side, and sits on the bench with her legs crossed.

"Holly, legs! Open. Them. Now," I grit out. She does, slowly, letting me see her smooth, wet pussy. Her lips are swollen; they're glistening with her desire. Even the camera can't hide how badly she wants this. "Are you in need of release, dolcezza?" I ask her.

"Shut up. You know I am. God, T, how have you managed to turn me on from the other side of the world?"

"It's a skill. Run your finger through your slit. Slowly."

She's hesitant, but her hands move as instructed. "T, someone will know."

"No one's going to know, except you and me, Holly. Hold your finger up. I want to see how wet you are for me." She lifts her hand towards the camera; it shines with her juices. "Mmm, fuck, I want to taste that!" I groan.

"Well, you can, anytime you want. Jump on a jet and come home, so you can taste it," she pleads.

"Soon, dolcezza, soon. I want to watch you. Position the camera right at your pussy, Holly. I want to watch your fingers ease the ache you're feeling."

"Argh, nothing is going to ease this ache until you're inside me again," she whispers.

"Holly, position the camera so I can see," I repeat more firmly.

"Why do I let you talk me into these things?" Even though she's questioning my intentions, she does as she's told.

"Fuck, that's the prettiest fucking pussy I've ever seen. Put your fingers on your clit and circle them." I watch as she draws little figure eights around the entrance of her pussy. Freeing my cock, I tug tight. I'm seconds away from coming, just watching her play with herself. "Put those two fingers inside, Holly, slowly. Ride your hand like it's mine."

"T, oh, God, I'm going to..." She gasps and moans

ever so quietly. I can see her pussy quivering as the orgasm runs through her, my own hitting me hard and fast.

"Fuck, you're goddamn perfect, Holly," I tell her in awe.

"And you're perverted. I can't believe I just did that in here." She picks up the phone, aiming it at her face—her *flushed* face.

She has that post-orgasm glow. I fucking love seeing her like this. Relaxed. Satisfied. I laugh. "Admit it. The idea of getting caught gets you off."

"No, *you* get me off." She's serious.

"I gotta go, Holly. Make sure you buy that set. And all the others. I want a collection of lingerie I can rip off you."

"Okay."

"And use the fucking cards I gave you."

"I don't need your money, T," she argues.

"I know you don't need it. And it's *our* money; we're married. Everything I have is yours."

"Mhmm, the only thing you have that I want right now is your body."

I feign a gasp. "And here I was, thinking you married me for my insanely charming personality."

Holly laughs. "I love you. Make sure you come home soon. In one piece."

"I'll be home soon. Love you." I hang up before I find a reason not to. I'm exhausted. I need to sleep so I can go into tomorrow head-on.

I wake to the sound of slamming. Jumping out of bed, I reach for the Glock under my pillow before I hear the arguing. "Fuck you, Alexei!" Lana yells.

"You already have, *this morning*, but if you want another go-around, be my guest." The Russian's voice, although nowhere near as loud as Lana's, carries through the villa.

Fucking hell... Why did I agree to let them stay here? I throw on a pair of sweats, tucking my sidearm into the back waistband as I walk out. "Some of us actually want to sleep, you know," I grunt, heading straight for the coffee pot—after all, the best fucking thing about Italy is the coffee. Oh, and the food of course.

"Don't worry, T, things are about to get real quiet around here when I kill this motherfucker." Lana points towards the man in question, while making no move to actually do him any bodily harm, though the same can't be said about the kitchen cabinets.

I look over at Alexei. "What'd you do?"

"Not a fucking thing," he grunts, before lowering himself onto the bench. I actually kind of feel bad for the guy—still fucking hate him—but I've been on the other end of Lana's temper. It's not pretty.

"Not a thing? Just tried to clip my wings after I finally broke free of my gilded cage. Do you think I'm going to willingly sign up to be someone's pet?" Lana spits out as she breaks eggs into a bowl.

I have no fucking clue what she's talking about. I look to Alexei for an explanation. "I asked her to marry me." He shrugs a shoulder, seemingly unfazed by his reluctant bride-to-be's *less than stellar* reaction.

"Okay, L, calm your ass down. If you don't want to marry the guy, just fucking say no. You don't have to wake up the whole goddamn neighborhood in the process." I lean against the counter and sip on the perfectly brewed liquid in my hands.

"Oh, but she said yes." Alexei smirks.

"He asked me mid-orgasm. I was already calling out yes." *Huh, that's actually a smart move.*

"Still a yes, milaya." Alexei smiles.

"No, I'm not *your sweetheart*. In fact, I'm not *your* anything right now, except maybe your potential killer. T, you'll help me bury the body, right?" She turns to me.

"Fuck no, your killing days are done, woman." I storm out of the room, the memory of my father choking to death replaying in my mind. Sometimes it's easy to fall back into old habits. We were best friends for so long. But I can't be Lana's friend anymore, not after what she did. I need to get out of here. Retreating to my room, I throw on some clothes and start making arrangements for meetings today. I'm one man. I can't fucking get this shit done alone. I'm going to need backup.

The sooner I get it sorted out, the sooner I can return to Holly.

I drive up to the gates, show the guard my face, and tell him my name. I watch as he speaks into a walkie-talkie before pressing a button and letting me through. I can spot three snipers, all with crosshairs pointed directly at me, as I pull along the tree-lined driveway. I send up a little prayer. I really fucking hope I make it out of here in one piece today. Parking off to the side, I decide to give Neo a call before I go in.

"Boss, what's good?"

"Fucking nothing. How's my wife?" I ask him.

"You know she has a phone, right? A nice little burner you gave her. Why don't you ask her yourself?"

"Because I'm fucking asking *you*. How's she doing?"

"Right now, she's out by the pool with Aunt Gloria, discussing wedding shit."

That makes me pause. Holly's discussing our wedding with my mother? Huh, I wonder when Ma came around to the idea of Holly being *good enough* for her baby boy. And if they're talking wedding plans, that means my mother knows I wasn't blown to pieces like everyone's supposed to think. "How the fuck does my mother know I'm alive?"

"*That*, you'll have to ask your wife."

"Fucking hell. Okay, look, I'm heading in to meet with Donatello now."

"What the fuck for? Alone?" I can hear his wheels turning as he tries to get one step ahead of the game.

"I'll fill you in when I make it out."

"*If* you make it out!" Neo yells. "This is crazy, T. Just get on the first fucking jet here. We can figure out another way—one that doesn't involve you going on a suicide mission."

"Relax, I'll be fine. Donatello is gonna wanna hear what I have to say."

"Don't leave me here to console your widow again. That was not fucking cool. Seeing that woman break made me actually want to kill you myself," he grunts.

"Are you going soft on me, coz? Maybe you're getting too close to my wife."

"Don't be an ass. You know it's not like that. But she's fucking impossible not to like and want to protect. Just hurry up and get home, so she can stop looking so fucking sad all the time."

"She's sad?"

"When she thinks no one is watching, she looks like someone just ran over her puppy."

"Okay, I gotta go. Just try to keep her busy. Keep her mind off shit, yeah?"

"Yeah."

I steel myself as I exit the car and walk up the steps, the double doors opening right as I go to knock. "Mr. Valentino. Welcome. Please, come in," a housemaid greets me. And the moment I step inside, I'm stopped by four armed guards. I smirk. They must be afraid of me if this is my welcome committee.

"Weapons in here," one says, holding up a plastic box. I look at the box and then back to him. Are they fucking nuts? Do they think I'm going to hand over everything?

"You either put your shit in here, or you can turn around and walk back out the fucking door," another says.

I smirk, drawing two Glocks from under my jacket. "Don't worry, I don't need these anyway. I can do enough damage all on my own." They stand there, in stony silence, as they watch me remove two more small-caliber pistols and three knives from various locations on my body.

"Follow me." The dipshit with the box ushers me forward. I don't waste time trailing behind. This isn't my first rodeo with some douchebag who thinks he's king shit. The guard knocks on a large oak door before holding it open for me to pass. Donatello is sitting behind a huge mahogany desk. What the fuck is it with these guys and mahogany desks? Is it in some sort of mob boss handbook or something? I must have missed that chapter.

"Valentino, I heard you got toasted," Donatello greets.

"I'm sure a lot of people will be disappointed to find out I wasn't." I hold out my hand to shake his.

His grip tightens before he lets go and points to a chair. "Have a seat. I was sorry to hear about your father. I apologize I couldn't get over there for the funeral. How's your mother doing?"

"Thanks. She's fine."

"I'm sure she is. Always was a tough one, that Gloria." Donatello's face flashes with... *something*. It's an odd look—a look I can't decipher.

I tilt my head and glare at him. "I wasn't aware you knew my mother that well."

"Oh, your mother and my sister went to school together. Anyway, what can I do for you? What brought you to my territory?" He's quick to change the subject. Interesting. I'm going to have to ask Ma what that's about.

I look around the room. There are two armed men at the door. I'm thankful Giovani isn't one of them. But those two need to go. "It's a sensitive matter." I cross my leg, resting my ankle on my thigh, and wait. Like I have nowhere else to be.

Donatello's gaze spears through me. If he's trying to make me squirm, he'll need to try harder. I don't fucking squirm for anyone. Finally, he nods his head, and the two soldiers disappear from the doorway.

"Now that you have my attention, Theo, what the fuck are you doing in Italy?"

Chapter Fifteen

Holly

I'm wading around in the pool with Gloria, drinking some of the best wine I've ever tasted. I couldn't hold it in any longer, and I ended up confessing to her that I've seen Theo, that I've spoken to him. She broke down and cried with relief. She understands this world of theirs a lot better than I do, because not once has she asked anything about why I didn't tell her sooner or why her son hadn't told her himself.

It's odd to me, how she just accepts it. Although, now that she knows for sure he's still alive, she's started planning our wedding. For someone who said (mere weeks ago) that I would never fit into their world, she's sure on board with me being her daughter-in-law.

I've started to tune her out a bit—you'd think she was planning a wedding for the royal family. I laugh at the thought. Then again, people do look at T like he's some sort of king. I can see it too: his appeal, how he commands a room with a confidence unlike anything I've ever witnessed before. I need to try to not think about him. The more I do, the harder it is to keep up with appearances. The heartbreak is too much. And if I'm not careful, I'm going to end up in a depressed hump, not able to shake myself out of it. I need to be thankful that he is alive, even if he's so far away from me right now. I wipe at a loose tear and dunk my head under the water.

When I come up, I'm met with Neo's stony gaze. "What's wrong?" he asks me as he stands at the edge of the pool, his arms crossed over his chest.

"You mean, besides the fact that my husband is on the other side of the world doing God only knows what, and I'm stuck here waiting and twiddling my thumbs with nothing more than a prayer that I'll actually see him again?" I pull myself out of the water and grab a towel. "I'm sorry, Gloria. I didn't mean that." I turn to her and apologize for my outburst.

"Yes, you did. And it's okay, darling. It's a lot to deal with. Trust me, I know." She pivots to Neo. "Where exactly is my son, and who is he doing business with?"

I can't help the snort that comes out. *Business.* Yep, let's just pretend that Theo is over in Italy on a regular *business* trip.

"Ah, I'm not too sure, Aunt Gloria." Neo squirms. Interesting. What is he hiding?

"Neo? Who's he meeting with? Why do you look so nervous all of a sudden?" I ask.

"Look, T's fine. I just talked to him. He's meeting with Donatello as we speak."

Gloria gasps before quickly schooling her features. "Donatello? Are you sure?"

"Yeah, why? He's fine. He's smart and more than capable of taking care of himself. You two need to stop worrying so much."

"I'll stop worrying when I have no reason to worry," I counter.

"Holly, darling, I'm feeling drained. I'm going to go lie down for a while. I'll see you at dinner. I've been cooking my special sauce all afternoon—you'll love it. I'll teach you the recipe one of these days." Gloria walks off in a rush.

Neo stares after her with a confused look on his face. "What the actual fuck? You're going to get that sauce recipe? She hasn't shared that with a single soul in all the years I've known her."

"Well, I guess she just hasn't had a wonderful daughter-in-law before." I smile, then drop it. "She *hasn't* had a daughter-in-law before, right? I mean, I should know if Theo has been married before... Why haven't I asked these questions until now?" I'm talking more to myself than Neo at this point.

"Holly, relax. You are literally the only woman for that man. He's never even thought of marrying anyone else."

"You mean, other than Lana," I say, not able to hide the jealousy in my tone.

"Nah, he was never going to go along with that. If L didn't stop *that* catastrophe, T would have found a way."

"Mmhmm." I walk inside. Maybe a nap is in order for me too. After a day of shopping and the extracurricular activities T coaxed me into doing, I'm exhausted.

I wake up in a dark room. I must have slept longer than I planned. Rolling over, I feel the emptiness of the spot next to me, and all of those negative feelings hit me at once. I went twenty-five years without sleeping next to someone (other than Reilly). Without *needing* someone next to me. How did everything change so quickly? How did I become so emotionally dependent on this man?

I swear I'm going to tie him to this bed when he actually comes home. I'm never letting him leave me again. I need some water. Or something stronger— something that will help me sleep through the night. I throw on one of Theo's shirts and exit the bedroom. The place smells like spaghetti, but not the crappy kind that I'd make. No, this kitchen smells like it's straight out of Italy, or what I imagine Italy would smell like.

Opening the fridge, I see a container with my name on it. I smile. Gloria must have set some aside for me. I can't believe I slept through dinner. I pull out the leftovers and pop them in the microwave. Then I spot an uncorked bottle of red wine on the bench, and after searching through four different cabinets, I finally manage to find a glass. It's not a wine glass, just an ordinary cup, but I'm not picky. I pour to the halfway point and take a sip. *Mmm, now THIS is wine.* I pick up the bottle and fill the rest of the glass. The beep of the microwave is loud, especially in the silence. I can hear crickets chirping outside. I turn around to grab my bowl and run straight into a brick wall.

"Shit, sorry. You good, ma'am?" Sonnie holds my arms to steady me.

"Ah, yeah. Sorry, I didn't hear you," I say, taking a step back.

"I heard some noise down here and wanted to make sure it wasn't a racoon." He smiles, though I don't miss the fact that he's tucking something into the back of his pants at the same time.

"We don't have racoons in Australia." I laugh.

"No, but you do have big-ass fucking spiders." He shudders.

"Aw, are you afraid of spiders, tough guy? Don't worry, I'll kill 'em all for you. It's easy. You just have to be fast."

"I don't know if you're being serious or not, but the next spider I see, I'm screaming out for you." He walks over and fills a glass with water from the tap.

"No worries, mate." I grab my bowl.

"You know, every man in this house tried to bribe Mrs. Valentino to get that last bit of pasta. Threatened she'd cut the hands off any of us if we even *thought* about touching it."

"Huh, I'm starting to like my mother-in-law more and more each day." I take a forkful of the pasta. "Oh my God, scratch that. I friggin' love her. Have you tried this?"

"Yep, I have. So, what's it worth to you? I'll give you a grand for it, *right now*," Sonnie offers.

I raise an eyebrow. "A grand? Sorry, but there isn't enough money in the world to make me give this up. There's only one thing I want, and no one here has it." Great, and now I'm back to the self-pity. It's like a pattern: something will briefly take my mind off things and then it's just a word, a smell, or a sound, and I'm back to thoughts of T.

"Don't worry, ma'am, he'll be home before you know it," Sonnie says.

"I sure do hope you're right." I guzzle down a mouthful of wine and pause. "So, I'm guessing you heard he's not dead?"

"I pay attention, ma'am. It's my job." He clears his throat. "Are you good here? I'm gonna head outside for a bit."

"Yeah, I'll be fine. I'm just gonna eat this and go back to bed."

I do go back to the bedroom, but I'm not alone. Nope, I have my new friend in tow. The delicious bottle of red wine I discovered. I'm on my second glass, and I'm already feeling the buzz. This is good; this is what I need to help me forget. I turn the television on and curl up in bed. And the first thing that comes on is a bloody Hallmark movie. Why is the universe out to get me? Can I just have five minutes of peace? Five minutes, without being reminded that my soulmate is literally on the other side of the world?

The phone rings. Great, now even he has a sixth sense. I consider ignoring it. Can I really pretend to be okay and happy right now? But then I remember... What if this is my last chance to talk to him? My last chance to tell him that I love him? I have to jump on that. "Hello?"

"Dolcezza, how are you? How's that wine?" His raspy voice sends shivers through my body.

"T, I thought I asked you... No, not asked, I told you to get rid of the cameras in this bedroom," I growl.

"I did, but I didn't get rid of the ones in the kitchen. Tell me, Holly, what were you talking to Sonnie about for so long?" He sounds pissed off.

"Oh, you know, all sorts of interesting things. The man's charming as hell, Theo. You really do know how to hire them. Or recruit them. Hang on, how *do* you find all of these people anyway?"

"Are you trying to sign the man's death certificate? Don't push me to do things you won't like, Holly, because I *will* cut his fucking balls off and force the fucker to eat them."

Huh, who would have thought he'd have such a jealous streak? Me. That's who. It was never a question. "Don't get your panties in a twist. We were talking about your mother's sauce. Do you have any idea how bloody amazing that stuff is? Sonnie offered me a grand for the last bowl." I laugh.

"I grew up on the stuff. Trust me, I know how good it is. It's the second-best thing I've ever tasted."

"Yeah? And what's the first?" I prompt.

"You," he says matter-of-factly.

133

"Riiiiight, well, did you have a reason for calling so late? I was about to watch a cheesy Hallmark movie and get all green with envy over fake people finding their happily-ever-afters, while I'm sitting in bed. By myself. Not knowing whether or not I'll ever get laid again in my life." The laughter that comes through the phone stops my ramblings. Why is he laughing at me? This is not funny. The prospect of never getting laid again is a serious matter. "Stop laughing. It's not a joke, T. How can I go the next sixty years without sex? Because that's what will happen if I never see you again. My vagina is going to shrivel up; it'll be covered in cobwebs and all."

"Holly, trust me. I promise you are going to get laid so fucking much over the next sixty years plus. You won't go a day without feeling my cock inside your pussy."

"Really? Well, I've gone about a week now, so I'm sure the cobwebs are already taking shape." I pout.

Chapter Sixteen

That wine has gone straight to her head, and a tipsy Holly is a *dramatic* Holly. I can't help but laugh at the fact that she thinks she's never going to get laid again. As soon as this shit's finished, she won't be able to walk straight. "Dolcezza, trust me, you're going to be seeing me again. Once this shit is handled, I'm taking you away. We're going to spend weeks on a deserted island somewhere, and

you'll get fucked in every possible position imaginable
—*I promise*."

"How long do you think this is going to last, T? I
really should get back to the school. The principal's
been lenient because he thinks my husband's just died,
though I'm sure it has more to do with Neo's *conversation* with him. But I do have to go to work, or I won't
have a job to return to."

"You don't need a job, Holly." I don't know how
many times I have to reiterate this to her. She's fucking
loaded. We have enough money that neither of us
would have to work another day in our lives, if we
didn't want to. That being said, the only way out for
me is a six-foot hole in the ground. You don't get to
walk away from the mafia... Being born into this family,
it's a fucking life sentence.

"I know I may not need one, but I want one. Also, I
have a work visa. I can't live in the States if I'm not
working, T."

Fuck, why the fuck didn't I think of that? I make a
mental note to have Neo start the process of getting
Holly a green card. He'll have it by the end of the
week. "Dolcezza, you're Mrs. Valentino. You can do
whatever the fuck it is you want to do. Live wherever
the fuck you want to live," I growl. I want her to realize
and *use* the power that comes with our shared last
name. I know it's not in her nature to throw her weight
around. But deep down, she loves it. She loved how she
felt when she pulled that trigger during target practice.

"Okay, well, my cup's empty now. I'm going to just lie down and go to sleep, thinking about all the sex I'm never going to have again," she huffs.

"Holly, go to sleep. I'll see you soon. I love you."

"Night, Theo. I love you too. Even if you are the reason my vagina is going to grow cobwebs." She hangs up before I can reply.

Fuck, I have to do something. I need to get back to her. Maybe I can disappear for a night. Donatello said something about the auction happening on Friday. That's a few days from now. If I leave soon, I can be in Sydney by tomorrow, spend a night or so, and fly back here Friday. I'm not sure what the fuck he's planning, but that's where the Clover will be. If I want to get anywhere near the Irish fuck, I need to be at that auction.

The only way to eliminate this ring is to chop it off at the head. And so far, everything I've learned points to the Clover being at the top. I send a text to my pilot, telling him to have the jet ready to leave for Sydney within the hour. Then I message Neo to let him know I'm on my way, but not to tell Holly. I want it to be a surprise.

I throw some clothes into a bag and walk out to find Lana and Alexei on the couch, clearly having made up. "I'm heading to Sydney. I'll be back Friday morning," I say.

"What for? And what happened with your meeting?" Lana asks, while Alexei tries to draw the answers out of me with his fucking stare. *Nice try, fucker.*

"I met him. We had whisky. I left. What's there to tell?" I shrug.

"No, you can't leave us out of this plan of yours, T. We came here together; you're not going into anything alone. Tell him, Alexei." Lana stares at her boyfriend, or is it *fiancé* now?

"I'm not telling him shit. If he wants to be a one-man show, let him. I'm only here because you are here," Alexei states calmly.

"Fuck off. We're doing this together. What is it, exactly, that we're doing, T?"

I count to ten, to try to find some fucking patience. "You wanna help bring down a sex trafficking ring, L? You're not doing shit; you're going to stay in this shit-hole villa until I get back."

"Why are you trying to bring down a sex ring?" Alexei asks, interested all of a sudden.

"Because these assholes are bringing this shit into my city. And I won't have women and children going missing from my streets or being fucking sold as slaves." This is something a lot of men in our industry either turn a blind eye to or get involved with in order to reap the profits. But me? I don't want any fucking part of it. I also can't pretend it isn't real. That it isn't happening.

"What do you mean *they're* bringing it into the city? Who are *they*?" he questions further.

I watch him, trying to figure out why he's asking. Is

he one of the fuckers involved in this shit? I wouldn't put anything past those fucking Russians. I tilt my head and smirk, even though the last thing I want to do is smile at this son of a bitch. "What's wrong, Alexei? Scared I might be ruining something you have a vested interest in?"

"Fuck off. We don't deal in slavery," he spits out. And for some odd reason, I believe him.

"Sure." I shrug. "This shit's organized by the Clover. Heard of him?" I raise an eyebrow. Everyone's heard of the fucking Clover.

"Are you fucking kidding me? You're going after the Clover? You're on a damn suicide mission, Theo." *Guess he's heard of him.*

"Aw, you're worried about me? Thanks, buddy. I appreciate the concern, but I'll be fine. Make sure you keep that one out of trouble while I'm gone," I say, pointing at Lana. As I walk out the door, I frown. What the fuck do I care if she gets herself into trouble? She's not my problem anymore. We're not friends, no matter how much she's trying to push herself back into my life.

I throw my bag into the SUV Donatello insisted I take after our meeting today. He mumbled something about it being bulletproof, and how I shouldn't be out here on my own in a shitty rental. I think he's probably got the thing bugged, and it's a way of keeping track of me. Although, when I ran a scanner over it, there was nothing. He also gave me a direct number and requested I let him know my plans before I acted on them.

Anyone else? Yeah, I'd tell him to fuck off with that shit. My father's dead, and I don't need some other asshole coming in and trying to tell me what to do. But this isn't just any old asshole. It's Donatello, and even I'm not stupid enough to test him. The five families may not answer to anyone back home. But here, in Italy, everyone answers to Donatello.

I'm halfway to the airport when I notice a car tailing me. A black SUV similar to the one I'm driving. I speed up, and sure enough, so do they. I pull out my phone and call Donatello. "T, didn't expect to hear from you so soon," he answers.

"Yeah, well, you wouldn't be if you didn't have fuckers following me. What the fuck are your guys tailing me for, Donatello?" I growl.

"I don't have anyone tailing you. Where are you?"

"I'm on the Autostrada A91, southbound, about twenty minutes out from the airfield. You're sure they're not your guys?" I ask, just as a bullet hits the back window. Fucking hell. "Good news: the glass really is bulletproof," I say.

"They're shooting at you?" Donatello yells through the phone, before cursing and issuing orders in Italian to someone else.

"Yeah, don't worry, not the first time I've been shot at. Probably won't be the last either."

"I have people close. You need to keep driving, T. Don't fucking stop."

"Yeah, wasn't planning on it," I grit out, while swerving into the other lanes. There's a loud bang and then the car is going sideways. Fuck, the fuckers shot out a back tire before ramming my bumper. "Ah, Donatello, might just want to send your cleaners out here. This is gonna get messy," I say, hanging up. The car finally comes to a stop. I jump over the passenger seat and exit that door.

Using the car for cover, I pop up and fire, getting the driver of the other car right between the eyes. *Good night, fucker.* I spot at least three others: one in the passenger seat and two in the back. Then I crouch down and count to ten, listening to their doors open and close. I dart back up and get one of them in the chest, but not before I take a bullet to the shoulder.

"Fuck, you're going to regret that, motherfucker," I yell out.

"Give it up, Valentino. You're outnumbered. You might want to make peace and say your last fucking prayers," some wanna-be thug spits out in Italian.

Yeah, not likely. I promised Holly she'd see me again, and I plan on keeping that fucking promise. I'm about to jump out and try to fire again, even though I have a bullet currently stuck in my shoulder (which fucking burns like all hell, by the way) when a chopper flies overhead. I see a fucking machine gun hanging out the side, then hear the sounds of the rounds hitting dirt, flesh, and metal, before the aircraft changes direction and hovers above me. For fuck's sake, is this what Donatello meant by having guys nearby? That's not just having guys nearby; he sent in the goddamn calvary.

I don't understand... But, fuck, I need to get out of here before the cops turn up. I reach in and grab my bag from the back seat, and just as I'm about to start walking the rest of the way to the airport, another fucking SUV pulls alongside me.

The back door opens. "Get in," Donatello orders. I look around. It's not like I really have any other options right now. "Who'd you manage to piss off already, T? You've been here all of what? Two days?"

"Fuck if I know? You should have more of an idea than I do."

"They won't come after you again. I'll make sure of it. Where are you headed?"

I'm curious as to why he'd *make sure of it*? He doesn't know me from Adam. Sure, he's heard of me, because he knew my father, but I can count on one hand how many times I've ever actually seen the guy. "Why? Don't get me wrong, I appreciate the help back there. But why do you care?"

"A favor to your mother. She called and told me some things I wasn't aware of. And let's just say I now have a vested interest in keeping you in one piece. How bad is it?" He nods towards my shoulder.

"I've had worse."

"Again, where are you headed?"

"Airport. I'm making a quick trip to Sydney."

"Leaving already? I thought you had more fight in you than that."

"I'll be back Friday morning. Like I said, it's a quick trip."

"What's in Sydney that has you runnin' there?"

"My wife," I say.

Donatello's eyes widen briefly. *Guess the news of my recent nuptials hasn't spread that far yet.* "I wasn't aware you were married. Congratulations. She must be special, for you to make a twenty-plus hour trip for what? One night, before you have to turn around?"

"She's worth it."

"Good, that's good." Donatello nods his head. "I'll have one of my doctors travel with you, so he can patch that up during the flight."

I'd like to refuse his help, to tell the son of a bitch that I don't want *or need* anything from him. But the truth is: I do need a fucking doctor to get this fucking bullet out of me. And the sooner, the better. "Thank you." I tip my head back and close my eyes. Holly's face is what I picture every time I do. I'll see her soon. That alone gives me the energy to keep going.

Chapter Seventeen

I'm going out of my damn mind. It's been exactly eighteen hours since I last spoke to T. Why hasn't he answered my messages? My calls are not even connecting. Neo doesn't seem to be worried, and that's a good thing. I think...

"Neo, you need to tell me where he is. Please, is he in danger? Is he hurt?" I plead.

"Holly, trust me when I say he's fine. He's just

busy. He will call you soon, I'm sure. Will ya please just calm down."

"No, I won't *calm down*. If he's so fine, then why the hell isn't he answering my messages? What if something bad happened? What if he needs me, and I don't know where he is? What if he's..." I can't bring myself to finish that thought.

"Holly, we'd know if anything happened to him. Believe me, the men in the mafia are bigger gossips than the fucking real housewives. News travels fast in our families. He is fine. You need to relax before *you're* not fine and get me shot, because you've given yourself a stroke from stress or some shit."

"Knock, knock. We're here," Reilly yells out as she enters the kitchen where I'm currently pacing.

"Thank fuck. What took you two so long?" Neo throws his hands in the air like he's giving up. "She's all yours. You fix her."

Reilly and Bray both laugh. "There's no fixing perfection, Neo, and Holly is bloody perfect. I dare you to say otherwise." Reilly raises an eyebrow at him. She's picked up just how much the men around me would do anything for me—anything but tell me where my bloody husband is.

"Of course she's perfect. Perfectly stressed."

"Holly, oh my gosh! Why didn't you tell me you were coming home?" My mum enters the kitchen.

I give Reilly the what-the-fuck look. I didn't want my mother to know I was here. How do I explain all of this to her? "Ah, hi, Mum. It was a quick trip. I'm not staying long." I struggle to get the words out as she wraps her arms around me.

"Well, I'm glad you're here. Dad's coming home next week. He will love that we're all together. I still can't believe it!" My mum runs her hands over my hair. It's a comfort I haven't felt in a long time, and I fight the tears threatening to escape.

Daddy's coming home? How did I let that slip my mind? "Yeah, it's a miracle, Mum," I agree, while looking at Neo. It's because of T... that's why my dad is coming home early. But I can't say that.

"Okay, now, tell me what this visit's really all about? And don't bullshit me, Holly Reynolds."

Gloria walks into the kitchen as my mother is scolding me. Great, now I have to introduce my mother-in-law to my mother, when I haven't even told my mother I have a mother-in-law in the first place. "Ah, Mum, I kind of met someone. Someone very special. Amazing. You're going to love him, because I do. So how could you not, right? He's caring, considerate, everything."

"Okay, so where is he?" My mum looks around, and her eyes land on Neo.

"Not me." He shakes his head.

"He's in Italy, on business, but he'll be meeting up with me here in a few weeks." I keep my voice calm, positive. Will he be meeting me here? I bloody hope so.

"Oh, okay. Well, that's nice. I'm happy for you. So,

will I get to meet this boyfriend of yours when he arrives?" Mum raises an eyebrow as she looks directly at my ring finger, where the huge bloody rock Theo put there still sits.

"Yeah, about that... I kind of got married." I hold up my hand like she hasn't already noticed the new jewelry. My mum stands there, in silence. She doesn't say anything, just stares for the longest time.

"Oh, shit, Hol, I think you actually broke her. Mum, you okay?" Reilly asks, stepping forward and waving her hands in front of our mother's face.

"What do you mean you got married? You were my last hope at actually planning a wedding for one of my daughters." Mum glares at Reilly, who just recently ran off to Vegas and eloped with Bray.

"Well, good news! Theo—that's his name, by the way—he still wants the big wedding. We were just discussing it this afternoon, weren't we, Gloria? Oh, and this is Gloria, Theo's mum. Gloria, my mum... Lynne." I introduce the two.

"It's lovely to meet you. You've raised quite a remarkable daughter, Lynne. We are very lucky to have her join our family." Gloria smiles, while Neo almost chokes on his drink.

Everyone turns to face him. "Sorry, went down the wrong way," he sputters.

"Anyway, Mum, why don't you stay here and chat about Holly's big day with Gloria. We're going out to the club for a few hours." Reilly pulls me away.

"Ah, no, Holly can't go to the club." Neo blocks the door.

"And why's that?" Reilly asks with a smile.

He looks to my mother; he can't say much with the current audience. "Because it's late, and she's tired." The excuse is lame, and even he knows it.

"Nice try. Now, move. We need to get ready. Don't worry, I brought a dress over for you," Reilly says.

Great, that means she brought me a scrap of fabric to wear.

What Reilly failed to mention was that she brought us *matching* dresses. We haven't worn matching dresses since we were kids… when we were *forced* to. "Seriously, Reilly? We look ridiculous." I pull at the extremely short, emerald-green, silk material—which is more like a negligee than an actual article of clothing. It's completely backless, the fabric sitting just under my ass.

"Speak for yourself. I look fucking fantastic. Bray is going to be extra hard all night." She winks.

"Not helping. Maybe I should just throw on a cardigan or something," I suggest.

"Nope, we're going. Come on. We're already late. Sarah is meeting us there. Alyssa is at home and probably sleeping. Remind me to never get knocked up. That shit doesn't look fun." Reilly laughs as we make our way downstairs.

"No fucking way! You're purposely tryin' to get me shot. Whichever one of you is Holly, turn your ass around, go back up there, and put some damn clothes on," Neo growls—yes, actually growls.

Bray chuckles and walks straight to Reilly, wrapping his arms around her. "You look fucking hot, babe. I might actually get to hit someone tonight."

I don't know how he does it, how he always manages to tell us apart, when we look exactly the same. "Hold up, how do you know that one's Reilly?" Neo asks.

"You really think I don't know my own wife?" Bray squints at him.

"Clearly you do," Neo mumbles. Then he turns to me. "Holly, please, for the love of God, put some fucking clothes on. T is gonna kill me when he finds out I've let you go out looking like *that*," he practically begs.

"Well, T isn't here, now, is he? And the only way he's going to find out is if one of you gossips tells him." I point from Neo to the other four men standing behind him quietly, all averting their eyes and trying not to look my way. "And besides, if T has a problem with how I dress, he can come here and tell me himself." That gives me an idea. I'm super pissed that he hasn't been answering my messages today. In actuality, I'm more concerned than pissed, but I'm trying to harvest the angry feelings so I don't break down. I grab my phone from my purse and hand it to Reilly. "I'm going to need a photo," I say as I pose seductively. I turn around with my back to the camera and pull my hair over one shoulder, while looking directly at the lens over the other. Then I part my lips in a small pout.

"Fuck yes!" Reilly cheers me on as she snaps away.

"I want black-dyed roses on my coffin." Neo sighs to Sonnie.

"Sure, boss, but you know we're all gonna go down for this, right?" He points to me. "Ma'am, are you sure you don't want to grab a coat or something?"

"It's thirty degrees Celsius outside. I don't need a coat. Stop worrying. T won't do anything to you. Despite what he may think, he's not the boss of me." I snatch my phone back and quickly fire off those images to Theo with the caption: *Heading to the club to dance the night away. If only I had a handsome man to accompany me...*

"He may not be the boss of you, but he sure as shit is the boss of us," one of the other guys mumbles loud enough for me to hear. I choose to ignore him. I thought they were all meant to be these fearless mafia soldiers, yet here they are, scared shitless because I'm wearing a dress that *might* be a little provocative. Okay, it's *a lot* provocative, and nothing like what I'd usually wear. But I'm not about to change now.

Why did I agree to this? Going out to nightclubs is Reilly's thing, not mine. It's loud, it's dark, and it's way overcrowded. I had a moment when I passed through the doors and froze. Neo walked straight into me, nearly pushing me over. He took one look at my face, grabbed my hand, and lead me to the VIP stairs ahead of the rest of our group. The bouncers at the top glared at me, then at Neo and our joined hands, before crossing their arms and frowning. That's when Reilly and Bray finally caught up, and the relief on the two men's faces was visible.

Neo sat me in one of the booths and had Sonnie order us some drinks. There was already an open bottle of champagne on the table, which Neo had picked up and discarded, muttering something about wanting *it sealed* and *not the cheap shit*—though I'm pretty sure that was an eight-hundred-dollar bottle. I know this because Reilly, Alyssa, Sarah, and I have polished off our fair share of that same label during our nights out together.

I keep checking my phone. It's been an hour since I sent T those photos, and he still hasn't replied. I'm officially scared. What if something bad has happened to him? And I'm sitting here. In a nightclub. *Drinking champagne.* Like everything is fine in the world...

I shudder at the thought as I glance to my left. Sarah is acting strange tonight (maybe it's just because I've been gone for a few weeks) but she doesn't seem to be her usual carefree self. I keep noticing her glare at Bray and Reilly whenever they kiss or make some other disgusting public display of affection, which is every other minute with these two. Then again, it could just be transference, passing my irrational thoughts and emotions onto her. I shake my head. I think I've officially had too much to drink. "Let's dance!" Sarah yells over the music. "That's what we came here to do, right?"

"Okay," I say, finishing the remainder of my glass. "Be a darl' and hold this for me." I hand my purse to Neo, who looks at it like it's going to jump out and bite him in the ass.

"Ah, no! If you're going down there, then guess what, buttercup? So are we." He turns and mumbles something to the four men standing at our table. They form a circle around Sarah, Reilly, and me as we head towards the dance floor. This has to be the easiest it's ever been to walk through a packed nightclub. Everyone shifts and makes room for us to pass. And if they don't move, they *get moved* by one of Neo's beefy goons.

"Okay, you are crowding me too much. Just go and stand over there. Nothing is going to happen to me on the dance floor," I say, and immediately stare at the exact spot I watched Bray get shot. Even in this dark, packed crowd, I can still see it.

"Holly, you are all right. Dance and have fun with your sister. But not as much fun as your friend there," Neo yells into my ear, while glaring over my shoulder.

I follow his line of sight. Sarah's already grinding on some random guy. Yeah, there's no chance of that happening. There's only one man I want to grind on, and he's not bloody here.

"I'm done. I need another drink, and I need to sit down!" I tell Reilly as she dances up against me.

Her eyes widen before her face lights up. "Oh, honey, your night is only just beginning."

That's when I feel it: the pair of hands gripping my waist. We've been on this dance floor for twenty minutes, and no one has so much as tried to come up and dance with us. But I don't need to turn around to know who's touching me. I can feel him. I look down, and sure enough, sitting on that left hand is the ring I put there. My heart is hammering in my chest.

Did I fall and knock myself out? Is this just some cruel dream I'm going to wake up from soon? I tentatively turn around and stare up into a pair of dark eyes.

His gaze runs up and down the length of my body before settling back on my face. The darkness is still there—it's always there—but more evident than that darkness right now is the lust.

"Are you really here?" I whisper.

He doesn't say anything. Instead, he holds my face in his hands, leans in, and claims my lips. And the moment we touch, everything else fades away. The music, the crowd, the stench of alcohol and sweaty bodies. It all disappears. Right along with that unnerving sadness that's been eating away at me. Having T's mouth on mine, being in his arms right now, it's like I can finally breathe again.

Tears roll down my cheeks. I'm pretty sure they're happy tears, or tears of relief. Because I know that he's okay, that he's in one piece. I pull back and take his hand. I need to get him alone. *And fast.*

Chapter Eighteen

I'm on my way to Holly when I get her text. *All of her texts.* I didn't have cell service in the air, and by the tone of her messages, she doesn't like my lack of response. Not one bit. But it's the last attachment that has my blood boiling. The photos she sent in some dark-green dress—not that I'd call that thing a fucking dress. What the fuck was she thinking, wearing that out in public? Better yet, what the fuck was *Neo*

thinking, *letting* her wear that out in public? Heads are going to fucking roll when I see them. She was headed to that nightclub her in-laws own. And she's already there, judging by the time stamp. "Change of plans. Take me to The Merge. You know it?"

The driver Neo sent to pick me up nods his head. "Sure thing, boss."

I should have gotten his name, but all I can think about is seeing Holly. And fucking covering up all of that delicious skin of hers. I call Neo to let him know I'm on my way. "Boss?" he yells. I can barely hear him over the music.

"I'll be there soon. Make sure no one gets within two fucking feet of her, Neo, or it's your fucking funeral. What the fuck is wrong with you? How could you let her out of the house like that?"

"Ah, not sure if you know your own fucking wife, but there is no telling that woman anything. What did you want me to do? Manhandle her? Lock her in a fucking room?"

Fucking hell, if any of my men touched her, they'd be staring at the other end of my Glock. Even my best friend. I really don't want to have to look for a new underboss, but if he were to force my hand, I'd choose her. Over anyone. Every fucking time. "Just keep her put until I get there. Think you can manage that?" I hang up without giving him time to reply.

"Here it is, boss. Need me to come inside with you?" The driver idles the engine in front of an impressive-looking building. Big marquee letters sit at the top. *The Merge.*

"No, I won't be long. I'm just picking something up." I exit the vehicle and make my way to the door, ignoring the line of people that runs around the corner of the block. The bouncers stop me with open palms. *Well, this is new. Guess we're not in Kansas anymore.* I've never—in my life—been denied access anywhere. I'm used to having the doors held wide fucking open for me before I even get to them. I size up the two steroid-induced meatheads. Do they actually think they can keep me out?

"The line's around the corner, mate," one of them says.

Mate? Really? I must be looking too fucking friendly these days. "I'm not you're fucking mate, and I'm not waiting to get into that club either." I smirk, waiting a beat before throwing a fist at the first guy. Then I toss up a knee and hear a rib or two crunch on impact. The bastard keels over and crumbles to the ground.

Right. Now it's time for meathead number two, who is currently speaking into his earpiece, probably asking for backup. I land a jab to his temple, and he goes down like a sack of shit. Huh, that was easier than I thought. I'm still fucking riled up though; all this pent-up energy needs a fucking release. Tugging at the sleeves of my jacket and straightening myself out, I push the doors open. I've seen a lot of clubs, but this is something else. Opulence at its finest. But I'm not here to admire the building or intriguing furniture. No, I'm here for one thing and one thing only. *My wife.*

It doesn't take me long to spot her. The fact that five of my men are surrounding her on the dance floor eases the task. I walk up to her. She's dancing with her sister; there are two of them. Why the fuck are they dressed the same? It doesn't matter. I know Holly is the one with her back to me. There is no mistaking the way my dick urges me forward with just one look at that ass.

Her sister's eyes widen when she spots me, then she smiles. I put my hands on Holly's hips, and it takes everything in me not to throw her over my shoulder and walk the fuck out of this place. If her dress wasn't so fucking short, I just might have. But if I picked her up as she stands, every fucker in a five-mile radius would win the lottery and get a glimpse of what that piece of fabric is doing a pathetic job of covering.

She takes a deep breath and her body sinks into me. It's fucking heaven. I finally have my hands on her again. Holly turns around and her eyes connect with mine. And I swear it's like she can see into the darkest parts of my soul, yet she stares back at me with love. If she truly knew the things I've done, the things I will continue to do, I'm not sure her love for me would be as strong. Who could actually love a monster? Holly's an angel, a fucking saint even, but everyone has their limits. I just hope she never finds *hers.* At least not when it comes to me.

I lean down and place my lips on hers. My hands tangle in her hair, while I hold her face still. I feel her tears hit my thumbs as she pulls back. Without a word, she takes my hand and ushers me forward. We get to an elevator and she hits the button. Turning back, she glares over my shoulder to Neo and the four other men he has with him. "You all need to stay up here," she says, pulling me into the elevator with her.

They look to me for direction, confused and unsure how to proceed. I give a simple nod of agreement. None of them seem all that happy about staying here, while Holly leads me away. What do they really think she's gonna do? I know what *I'm hoping* she'll do, and that involves her lips wrapped around my cock. Or her pussy milking me for everything I've got.

The doors close, and I quietly watch as she types a number into the keypad. The elevator starts to descend. The moment she turns around to face me, I pick her up, ignoring the burn in my shoulder. I press her back against the wall, and our mouths crash together as she wraps her legs around my waist. The sound of the doors opening again has me pulling away from her slightly, as I walk out with her still in my arms. I look around. We've entered a long cement hall-way. "What is this place?" I ask.

"It's the basement... where Bray used to fight. Second door, go there," she instructs. I stalk forward and open the second door, stepping into an empty room. Not the best accommodations... But right now, all I need is Holly, and maybe a hard surface to hold her up against. She reaches out and kicks the door shut. "How is this possible? How are you here?" Her voice is like a whisper.

"My wife complained she wasn't getting laid enough. What kind of husband would I be if I didn't find a way to rectify that?"

"So, you flew across the world... to what? Have sex?"

"No, I flew across the world to utterly and thoroughly fuck you, dolcezza. I'm going to make sure you'll still feel me next week."

"Mmm, well, what are you waiting for? Less talking and more doing, T." She doesn't have to tell me twice. I place Holly back on her feet and peel the straps of her dress down and over her shoulders. The flimsy material pools by her ankles, and she's left standing there in heels and a pair of dark-green panties. Fisting the lace in my hand, I tear one side of them and watch as they flutter to the floor. Holly gasps and glares at her now-ruined undergarments. "I liked those," she pouts.

"I'll buy you more." My eyes rake up and down her naked body. I'm not sure where I want to start. Every inch of her is fucking perfection. And then she drops to her knees. Her lips tilt up as she reaches for my belt, unlooping it before unbuttoning my pants. Her tiny hand reaches in and pulls out my cock. "Argh. Fuck,

Holly, you're so fucking hot right now," I groan as her palm pumps my shaft.

"You have no idea how much I've wanted to do this lately." She leans in, running her tongue along the length of my cock, before twirling it around the tip and lapping up the precum that's already dripping out. "Mmm, I love tasting you."

"Nope. Up. Now!" I pull her to her feet, spin her around, and prop her against the closest wall. "I need to be buried inside you now. Are you ready for me, dolcezza?" I wait until she nods her head, then enter her with a quick thrust. "Fuck!" I yell out as I still. I know she needs time to adjust to my size. My lips make their way to her neck and nibble on her ear. "I missed you so fucking much. I didn't think it was possible to miss anything this much."

"Mmm, T?"

"Yeah?"

"Fuck me already, please."

Yes, ma'am. Drawing out briefly, I thrust forward again, and her head falls back as I bottom out inside her. As much as I want to fuck her hard and fast, I need to go slow, otherwise this will be over sooner than I want it to be. If I had it my way, I'd stay buried inside her forever, never leaving my happy place between her legs. "I fucking love your pussy. It's goddamn perfect. You are fucking perfect." My thrusts quicken. "I need you to fucking come, Holly."

"You and me both. Oh, God!" Her legs tighten

around my waist. Creating a bit of space between us, I reach a hand down and find her clit. "Yes, T. That. Don't stop. I'm going to…" She screams out as her hips meet mine, thrust for fucking thrust.

"Fuck, I love how you soak my cock. You're so fucking wet. And it's all mine." I bite down on the soft skin of her neck, and she detonates. Her moans echo against the concrete walls. My body tightens as the tingles run up my spine, my balls constrict, and I come undone, painting the depths of her pussy with my seed. Fuck, I think I needed that more than I was willing to admit. How the hell did I think I could go weeks without her? I was a fucking idiot. Holly makes my whole world better. Brighter. She's obviously way too good for me, but she's mine. And that's never changing. "Well, that was quite the welcome home, Mrs. Valentino."

I pull out, groaning at the loss of her warm, wet pussy wrapped around my cock. I tuck myself back into my pants and refasten my belt, while taking my fill of Holly's naked, thoroughly fucked body standing in front of me. Her face has a nice red hue to it, and her eyes are glazed over in post-orgasmic bliss. It's a good fucking look on her.

Chapter Nineteen

Holly

I can't move. I'm standing here, catching my breath while watching T put himself back together—he's tucking away that bit of anatomy he uses so bloody well on me.

I'm overcome by several different emotions at once. I don't know how to process the feelings hitting me like a freight train. I'm ecstatic that he's here, I'm coming down from one hell of an orgasm, and I'm pissed off that I had to go without him for so long. But most of all, I'm terrified because I know he's not here to stay. I know he'll be leaving again, and I don't want to have to deal with another goodbye. I wonder if I can figure out a way to hide out in his jet, be a stowaway or something, and just follow him back to Italy.

Thoughts of handcuffing him to a bed, locking him in a basement, and saying to hell with the rest of the world are becoming more appealing by the minute. He's mine. I don't want to have to share him with his job. It's selfish, and I know that neither of us have the luxury of choice when it comes down to it. He's made it very clear: *there's no way out.* Thousands of people rely on him. Even if he didn't want to be the head of the family, which he tells me he does, he has been groomed for the position since the day he was born.

I watch as he plucks my ripped panties from the floor and tucks them into his pocket, before picking up my dress. "I hate to cover up such a masterpiece, but I'm the only one who gets to appreciate this opera d'arte."

I feel myself growing wetter at his use of Italian. The bastard smirks. He knows what it does to me, even if I have no idea what he's saying. He literally could be telling me I look like a toad, for all I know. "What does that mean?" I ask, holding my hands up as he slips the dress over my head.

"Work of art. Your body is a fucking work of art, Holly."

I have no words. How does someone reply to a compliment like that? "Thanks?"

"No need to thank me, dolcezza. I'm the one who should be thanking you. Fucking worshiping you. A guy like me isn't supposed to end up with a girl like you, Holly. The fact that you haven't tried to run as far and as fast as you possibly can yet is a miracle."

"Run? Tell me, Theo, where could I possibly go that you wouldn't find me?" When he wants to find someone, Neo has their location within the hour— usually less. I've seen it myself firsthand, and heard it during conversations I wasn't meant to be eavesdropping on.

Theo's face clouds over, his brow furrows, and his lips draw back. "Do you want to run, Holly? Do you want a way out of this?"

Okay, he's officially insane if he thinks I want to run from him. I shake my head and wrap my arms around his neck. "I don't want to run from you, Theo. I want to bloody run *to* you. Just minutes ago, I was trying to figure out how to make myself a stowaway on your jet, so I could follow you to Italy. I don't like being away from you. No, I fucking hate it. I fucking hate going to bed at night without you. I hate reaching over, only to find your pillow empty each morning. You got me hooked on you, and then you left. That's not fair." By the time I've finished my tirade, I've untangled myself from him. This conversation has me seeing red. Do I want to run? What kind of question is that? He's standing there with a huge grin on his face. "What are you smiling about?" I ask, folding my arms over my chest.

His eyes drop with the motion, taking me in before they lift to meet mine, and he shrugs a shoulder. "You're fucking adorable when you curse, dolcezza."

"Shut up! I am not!" I smack a hand against his shoulder to shove him back a little. He winces, hiding it fast, but not fast enough. "What's wrong? What happened?" I ask, reaching up to take his jacket off, and gasp. "What the hell happened? T, you're bleeding."

He grabs my hands to stop my movements. "Holly, it's fine. I just tore a stitch during our little reunion here. Trust me, it was fucking worth it."

"It's not fine. You're bleeding. Why do you have stitches anyway?" I'm staring at the red-stained shirt as I wait for him to answer. When he doesn't, I look up and meet his eyes. His jaw is tensed and his lips are thinned out. "T, what happened? Why'd you need stitches? And don't even think about lying to me."

"I can't tell you that, dolcezza. But it's fine. I'm okay. You don't need to worry."

"You *can* tell me; you just don't want to." My eyebrows draw down. "Do you not trust me?"

"Holly, I trust you more than anyone. You are my person—you know that."

"Well, then tell me what the fuck happened!" I yell.

He takes a deep breath. "I caught a bullet in my shoulder on the way to the airport yesterday. It's fine. I'm fine. I don't want you to worry about me." He tries to wrap his arms around my waist. I shake him off.

"You were shot? What the hell? Who the bloody hell shot you?" *Now, I'm furious.* I want to fly to Italy and shoot someone—see how much they like it. I also want to bloody castrate Theo for not telling me sooner. And for acting like this isn't a big deal.

"Holly, calm down. I'm okay. I'm standing right in front of you. In one piece. Trust me, I came out better than the other guys."

I huff, pulling the door open. "Follow me," I throw over my shoulder. I know Zac keeps a first aid kit in his office and probably a spare shirt I can borrow.

"Lead the way. I'd follow you into the depths of hell, dolcezza."

"Not the time to be cute, Theo Anthony Valentino."

He mumbles something I don't quite catch—not that I care to hear whatever it is he has to say at the moment. I stab my finger on the button that will lead us up to the offices. "Ah, Holly, where exactly are you taking me?"

"To Zac's office. He has a first aid kit, and you need to do something about that shirt, before I take you back into the club to show off my insanely freaking hot husband to everyone."

"Holly, I'm fine. I'll get it looked at once we're home."

I choose to ignore him and step out of the lift. I know he'll follow. When I reach the office door, I don't even bother knocking. I swing it open. Thank God it's unlocked. My steps falter when I'm met by Zac's unimpressed glare. "Does no one in this family know how to fucking knock on a door?" he grumbles.

I can feel T tense up behind me. Before he can jump to my rescue and do something he can't undo, I walk inside. "Hey. Sorry. I wasn't expecting you to be here, Zac. I won't be long. I just need a first aid kit. Do you have one?" I use the sweetest voice I can muster.

Zac might try to come across like a grizzly bear, all claws and teeth. But deep down, I know he's just a big, soft, cuddly teddy bear, who will do anything for his family. And somehow, I've managed to make it into his inner circle. He stands quickly and rounds his desk. "What's wrong? Are you hurt? Did someone do something to you, Holly?" Although he's asking me, he's looking directly at T.

"No, I'm fine. It's not for me. Oh, and this is Theo. My *husband*," I enunciate the last word and watch the momentary shock appear on Zac's face.

"I see." Zac looks back to me, ignoring Theo's presence entirely. "Are you sure you're okay? If you need help, Hol, just say the word."

"I'm fine. I just need a first aid kit, before he bleeds out in your office. Oh, and maybe a spare shirt."

"Sure, it's in the bathroom. What happened? I saw what *your husband* did to my bouncers at the door. It didn't look like they got a single shot in, so why is he bleeding out in my office?"

I turn to Theo. "What did you do to the bouncers?"

He smirks at me. "They weren't going to let me in. I just ensured they wouldn't make that mistake again."

My eyes bug out of my head. "T, this isn't New York. You can't just come in here and... I don't know... but you just can't."

"And yet I did." He looks to Zac. "Sorry about your bouncers, but you probably need to find yourself some better security."

"Perhaps," Zac replies. Then he opens a door and pulls out a white shirt. They look roughly the same size; it should fit okay. "So, what happened between the front door and you two going down to the basement?"

"It's just a scratch. Holly's overreacting."

I stare at T. Is he serious right now? *I'm overreacting?* I go into the bathroom and dig out the first aid kit from the cabinet. "Take off your shirt," I demand. "And sit down on the couch."

"Yes, boss." He laughs as he shrugs out of his jacket and unfastens the buttons of his now-ruined white business shirt.

"Just a scratch, huh?" Zac returns to his seat behind the desk.

When I see the gash and the ripped stitches on

Theo's shoulder, I can't help the tear that escapes. He was shot. Someone pointed a gun at him and pulled the trigger. My hands shake as I wipe the blood away. It's not bleeding as much as I thought.

T takes hold of my wrist. "Dolcezza, look at me." He waits for me to lift my face to his. "I'm okay. I'm fine."

"Theo, someone shot you. You're not *fine*. Someone actually wanted to kill you. That's not okay," I say.

"Well, it's nothing I haven't managed before. Call it an occupational hazard. But trust me, right now, I'm okay."

"I want to fly to Italy and burn the whole country down. Whoever thinks they can go after you obviously doesn't know that you're mine."

T leans in and kisses me gently, keeping it very PG. "I fucking love you."

"I love you more when you don't have bullet wounds, so try to stay in one piece."

I hear Zac's chuckle, which stops the moment I turn my glare on him. "You look way too much like your sister with that scowl on your face. Reilly is the mean one, remember? You're meant to be the sweet, nice one, Holly."

"Are you saying my wife isn't sweet and nice?" T questions, ready to jump to his feet. I push him back against the sofa.

"Sit down. Ignore him." I look over at Zac. "Do you

really think I don't know how to be mean, Zac? I grew up right alongside Reilly. Every bit of trouble she got into, I was there with her. Don't forget that."

"Wouldn't dream of it. Speaking of the little troublemaker, three, two, one..." Zac motions towards the door as it opens and slams against the wall.

"Zac, I can't find Hol..." Reilly's words drop off as soon as she spots me. "What the fuck happened? Holly, are you okay? What'd he do to make you angry?" Then she stalks over, looking Theo up and down as she whispers, "Damn, I can see why you signed those marriage documents now." I know by the tilt of T's lips that he heard her too.

"Shut up." I shove her out of the way and tape gauze over the popped stitch, before throwing the new shirt at Theo. "Put this on. There is no way you're walking down there without a shirt." He raises an eyebrow, and I know what he's thinking. "I have a dress on," I answer his unspoken question.

"Barely," T and Zac both mumble at the same time.

"Okay, why didn't you all tell me the party moved up here?" Bray hollers from the doorway.

"What happened?" Reilly asks again, nodding her head towards Theo. It occurs to me that Reilly and Bray haven't even officially met him.

"Oh, this is T, by the way. My husband. T, my very annoying sister, Reilly, and her very obsessed husband, Bray." I point between them.

"Don't think just because you're bleeding, you're

getting away with the fact that you went and married my sister without even telling me first. I mean, she didn't even have a dress, and I should have been there. I don't care if you're meant to be this big, bad mafia boss or whatever, I will find you and tear you to pieces if you ever hurt her." Reilly says all of this, then smiles. "Hi, I'm Reilly. It's nice to finally meet you."

Theo looks from me to her with questions he's not stupid enough to ask right now. He holds a hand out to shake hers. "It's nice to meet you too. And you don't have to worry. I'd never hurt a hair on my wife's head."

I roll my eyes. I swear he loves to say "my wife" in a sentence as often as he can. Does he think anyone's likely to forget? I sure as hell won't. Once T has finished his exchange with Reilly, he steps to Bray and offers a palm. Bray shakes it, and they share some kind of weird, unspoken man-head-nod thing. "Okay, so now that you're all patched up and shit, there's drinking to be done." Bray saunters over to Zac's mini bar.

"Bray, get the fuck out of my office. Some of us actually have work to do. In case you forgot, there are three bars downstairs. Go and drink from one of them."

"Okay, bro, don't get your knickers in a twist. Ignore him. He's just cranky because he had to actually leave his wife's side for a few hours and come to work." Bray takes Reilly's hand as he walks back towards the lift.

"Thank you for letting me use your office, and

sorry for interrupting you." I pack up the first aid kit and return it to the bathroom.

"Holly, you're welcome here whenever you need anything. You know that." Zac drops his gaze to his computer screen, tapping furiously at the keyboard.

"Well, I appreciate it," I say. "Let's go before those two come looking for us again."

"Thanks, man, I'll have someone replace your shirt tomorrow," Theo tells Zac.

"No need. It's Bray's." Zac laughs as we exit the office and make our way towards the club.

Chapter Twenty

"Argh, God, why?" Holly croaks out, her voice hoarse from sleep as she slaps a hand over my chest.

I take hold of her wrist before she hits any higher and lands on my fucking shoulder. That fucker still hurts like hell. But I'll never admit that to her. It would only cause unnecessary concern. I bring her fingers to my lips and kiss each one. "Is someone maybe regretting the amount of alcohol she consumed last night?" I laugh.

"Shhh, don't yell. It's too loud." She buries her face against me, pulling the blankets up to her chin.

I run a hand over her head, stroking my fingers through her hair. I fucking love her hair. "Dolcezza, want me to get you some Advil or some water maybe?"

"No, don't move. You're my pillow. You can't move."

"Okay, but you should hop up and eat. Getting some food and some aspirin into you will make you feel ten times better."

"Oh, God, no!" she groans as she stands and runs to the bathroom. I'm quick to follow. I kneel beside her, pick up her hair, and hold it away from her face as she offers the contents of her stomach to the porcelain gods. After a few minutes, she slumps back and rests against the wall. "Don't look at me. You should not be seeing me like this. I'm gross. You're never going to want to have sex with me again. Oh, God, my life is officially over."

"Holly, there is nothing that would ever make me not want to have sex with you. Trust me on that. I'd still fuck you even if you had an alien tearing its way out of your stomach, looking to bite my dick off."

She squints her eyes at me in disgust. "Where do you come up with this stuff?"

"It's a gift. Here, take these." I hand her two pills and a cup of water. She reaches out with a huff and pops the medication into her mouth, as I run the shower and check the temperature. "Come on, stand up." Then I gently tug her to her feet, remove her shirt, toss it to the side, and lead her under the water.

"Mmm, that's good." My cock jumps at hearing her moan, even if the sound has nothing to do with me and everything to do with the massaging showerhead.

"Tip your head back." I wet her hair before pulling her back out of the water. Reaching behind her, I squirt her shampoo into my hands and lather it into her scalp.

I should make it a rule that I wash her hair every time we shower. As I'm massaging her roots, she rests her head on my chest and leans into me. "You're too good to me, T. Why are you so good?"

"You make me want to be good, dolcezza, but you deserve so much more than what I can give you." I kiss her forehead.

She snorts—yep, snorts. "You have given me every-thing. And the sex... well, you're really good at that. Like freakishly good. And you're always so damn charming. You make my heart swell. I'm proud to be your wife, Theo."

"Good, because you're the best fucking wife I've ever had."

"I'm the only wife you've ever had, right?"

"Yes, Holly, of course you are."

"Okay, good."

"Can we stay here and pretend the rest of the world doesn't exist for just one more hour?"

After I washed her hair and thoroughly scrubbed her body, we came back to bed. Holly snuggled into my side, wrapping herself around me, and hasn't moved since. That was two hours ago. "Someone's going to bust the door down soon if we don't get out there," I say. Every thirty minutes or so, I've had fucking Neo either knocking on the door or sending me a text— apparently checking to see if I'm still alive.

"Neo made me put a gun in the bedside drawer. Just shoot anyone who comes in."

"You don't mean that, dolcezza." I laugh.

"Yeah, probably not. What are you going to say to your mum?"

"What do you mean? What do I need to say to my mom?"

"She was heartbroken, T. You let her think you were dead. Do you have any idea what that does to a parent? No, of course you don't."

"Holly, Ma will be fine. She understands that sometimes we have to do things we don't want to do, for the greater good of the family. She's not going to ask questions."

"Mmm." She rolls off me and out of bed. I watch her throw on a white sundress. Her hair has dried out a bit and hangs in waves down her back. Fuck, she's gorgeous. "I need coffee. If you'd like to grace us all with your presence, your highness, I'm sure your family would appreciate seeing you." She walks out of the room, slamming the door behind her.

I wonder if it's just me, if I'm the only one who manages to piss her off all the time, or if she's always been this feisty. She's nothing like the shy girl I saw in the café that first night—the one too afraid to look up and meet everyone's stare. No, now she's a goddess, someone even I'd think twice before crossing. I smile as I drag my sorry ass out of bed. I walk into our shared closet, fully stocked with enough clothes for both of us.

I enjoy seeing our worlds coincide like this. All of our shit in one place, together. I have one more night here before I have to get back on the jet to Italy. And right now, leaving Holly again is the last thing I want to fucking do.

As soon as I walk into the dining room, Ma jumps up and hugs me in the way only a mother could. She doesn't say anything as I return her embrace. When she pulls away, her hand comes out and slaps me across the back of my head. "Ow, fuck. Ma, what was that for?"

"For making your poor wife think you were dead. Don't ever do that to her again, Theo. Now, come and eat. I can feel your ribs."

I look around the dining room. Neo sits across from Holly, and Sonnie sits to her left, while the spot at the head of the table is empty. There are four of our other men joining us as well. What the fuck is going on? They're here to do a job, to protect my wife and make sure no one gets into this house. Why are they sitting around like it's the goddamn last supper? Everyone is staring my way, waiting for me to either say something or take my seat.

I look to Holly. *This was her doing.* She's made friends with the soldiers. Of course she has. Neo should have put a stop to that. "T, did you know your mum makes the best pancakes? Like seriously, how are they this fluffy?" Holly smiles.

"Thank you, dear, I'll show you the recipe," Ma says.

"What fucking twilight zone did I wake up in?" I throw the question to Neo, as I lean down and kiss Holly's forehead before taking my seat next to her.

"Don't fucking ask. She even got the sauce recipe, man. The fucking sauce recipe. I'm gutted, Aunt Gloria. I've always been your favorite, and just like that, you went and replaced me with this one." He waves his fork in Holly's direction, and the corners of her lips tilt upwards.

"Nobody likes a crybaby, Neo. Get over it. Or better yet, go and find yourself a nice wife like Holly here, and I might pass the recipe on to her." Ma laughs.

"Well, considering my girl is one in a million, Neo doesn't stand a chance."

"So, how long are you here for, Theo? Did you get everything in Italy sorted out?" I'm taken aback by my mother's sudden change in conversation. Not once in my whole life have I ever heard her ask my father anything about the family business.

I want to tell her that it doesn't concern her. It's on the tip of my tongue, to remind her that it's business and business does not concern wives. That's what I was brought up to believe anyway. But then I look at Holly's expectant face. She's keen to know the answer too. I won't tell them everything, but I can give them something. "I'm flying back out in the morning. I'm hoping only another couple of days on the mainland, and then we can all go home."

"Great. I've never been to Italy. Gloria, I'm sure you can show me so many sites while T's busy work-ing. Oh, what's the weather like? What should I pack?" Holly asks excitedly.

"Dolcezza, you're not coming with me," I state, and take a mouthful of pancakes.

"Oh, okay." Holly pulls out her phone and taps away. "Sorry if this is rude, but I won't be long." She puts the phone to her ear and waits. We all sit and watch, wondering what the hell she's doing. "Hey, Dean, it's Holly. Actually, hold on a sec. I need to put you on speaker; my hands are full." She taps the button and lets everyone at the table listen in. I already know who she's called. Dean McKinley, one of her brother-in-law's friends. What I don't know is *why*. "I need a lift somewhere. You know I wouldn't usually ever ask this, but it's urgent, and I don't know anyone else who can help."

"A lift? Sure, where you at, Hol? I'll come get you." Dean, the fucker, sounds all too fucking happy to pick her up.

"Well, that's the thing... I don't need the car kind of lift. I need to borrow your jet. I need to get to Italy. Tomorrow, if it's possible. I can pay you, of course." I'm speechless. What the fuck is she thinking? She's not getting on anyone else's fucking jet.

"Ah, yeah, okay. Let me send a message and make sure my brother isn't out of town. But even if he is, I'll get him to send the jet back for you. What time tomorrow? And you're not fucking paying anything. You're family, Hol. If you ever need anything, all you have to do is ask," the fucker says.

Fuck that. I reach over, grab the phone out of her hand, and hang it up. "You are not getting on his fucking jet. Forget it."

"That was rude," Holly says, snatching her phone back. "See? I don't need your permission to do shit, T.

You are not the boss of me. If I want to go to Italy, I damn well will go to Italy. If I want to take your mother to Italy, guess what? I will take your mother to Italy. If I want to do something, anything, in Italy, I will find a way to do it. *In Italy*. With or without you." Her phone starts ringing in her hand, and she smiles. "Oh, look, he's calling back. Should I tell him to have his jet fueled for me, or are we going in yours?" she asks with a smile.

Fuck! I turn to Neo for help, but he holds his palms in the air. "I'm staying out of this."

"Fine. I'll take you to Italy." I jump up and throw my napkin on the table. "Neo, I want thirty extra men to meet us at the airfield when we land. And we'll be going to the Valentino estate. Make sure everyone is aware we're coming—they're to be on high alert." I walk out of the room.

My heart is racing; my palms are sweaty. I don't like the thought of taking Holly with me. She should stay here. She's safer here. I need to do something to expel this built-up energy. I head down to the basement gym. I've only been lifting for five minutes when I feel her presence. I watch her approach. She's nervous.

Good, she should be after that fucking stunt she just pulled.

Chapter Twenty-One

Holly

Shit, I might have just pushed T too far. I don't think I remember a time when I've seen him this angry at something I've done. I don't know what came over me. When he flat-out said I wasn't going to Italy, I panicked. The thought of not being with him, of him leaving me again... I just couldn't accept it. I would have spent every last dime in my trust account to find a way to follow him. Wherever he is, that's where I want to be too. I can't handle the thought of being away from him. I don't want oceans between us. I don't even want a meter between us. And now I've gone and shown him just how much of a crazy stage-five clinger he's made me become.

It's his fault, really. I've never needed anyone like I need him. Just the thought of him leaving has my skin itching and my heart racing. It's not healthy. I know that, but I can't stop these feelings. I'm assuming it has something to do with being made to think he was dead for those three days. That's not something I ever want to experience again. Maybe I'm just not over how it felt to have my whole world taken away from me yet. I'm sure I could keep a psychologist in business for years with how messed up my head is right now. I don't even want to think about how much my dad coming home is adding to the mix.

Shit, I should visit him. I haven't been there in years, because I couldn't handle seeing him that way. But he's getting out in a few days. I'm sure he'll expect to see me, and I won't be here. Because nothing is stopping me from boarding that jet. I need to find T and let him know I'm going to visit my dad. I also don't like that he's angry at something I've done.

After walking around the top floor of the house, I head downstairs and find him in the gym. I stand still for a moment in order to fully appreciate the view. He's taken his shirt off and he's pressing weights. Someone get me a cold shower. I'm at risk of jumping him here and now. All those muscles on display and those tattoos his suits hide so well... Right now, he looks every bit the bad boy he really is.

And I want him. The question is: does he still want me? Or did I finally fuck this up? I've been waiting for the other shoe to drop, so to speak. Or to wake up from a vivid dream, only to realize that this, that Theo, isn't real—though it's needless to say that in this moment he looks pretty freaking real. I walk towards him tentatively. My eyebrows furrow as I notice he's ripped his stitches again. We just had the doctor here late last night suturing him back up. I have no idea where they found a doctor to do a house call at that hour. But I didn't question it, because I wanted him taken care of.

"T, you need to stop. You're bleeding again," I say quietly.

"I don't care about the fucking stitches, Holly." He continues to pump the weight bar up and down.

Okay, so definitely still mad. Great, what the hell am I meant to do? I stand there for a while, until I decide that I don't actually have *to do* anything. If he has a problem, then that's up to him to get over it, *not me.* "I just came in to tell you that I'm going to visit my father. Please don't leave before I come back." I want to make him promise that he'll wait. But I won't do that. I won't beg.

I hear metal clanging together as I turn to walk out. "You are not going to a fucking prison by yourself, Holly."

"Oh yeah, and who's going to stop me?" My hands rest on my hips.

T pops up and stalks—yes, bloody stalks—towards me with a look that I'm sure has a lot of people begging him for mercy. I step back, my legs hit a bench seat, and I fall on my ass. I now have Theo standing above me while he eyes me like I'm his prey. He bends down, placing his palms flat on each side of my thighs. "I think you're underestimating the measures I'm willing to take in order to ensure your safety, dolcezza." I suck in a huge breath, but I don't say a word. *What can I say?* "Don't think I won't lock you away in a room somewhere. When all's said and done, I can live with you hating me, Holly. But I cannot live *without* you. So, don't push me into a corner. You won't like the outcome."

The last thing I should be right now is turned on, right? My panties should not be wetter than ever before. I should be mad. I should tell him where to shove his overprotective, condescending ass. That's not what I want to do though. Nope, not even close. My hands go to his hair, and I drag his face down the extra twenty centimeters to close the space between us.

Theo picks me up, and spinning around, he sits on the bench seat with me straddling his lap. "Don't think this means we're done with this conversation, dolcezza. We *will* be talking about your apparent lack of safety awareness." He rips my dress over my head, and I'm left in a matching white bra and panties. I'm about to tell him not to rip them when he reaches down and tears through the lace. I roll my eyes. At this rate, he might as well buy a Victoria's Secret franchise. "This..." He places his hand over my pussy. "...is mine. These..." He cups both of my breasts, tugging on the lace material to release them. "...are fucking mine." His fingertips trail down the sides of my stomach. "Every fucking perfect inch of you is mine. And I will not have anyone, you included, disregarding the safety of something that belongs to me."

"Mmhmm, you do know that I've visited my father in jail before, without you or your security team."

"That was *before* you were mine," he murmurs into my neck as he thrusts two fingers into me. "I take care of my things, Holly."

"Mmhmm, I'm not opposed to you taking care of me right now." I grind down on his hand. T's tongue licks along the length of my collarbone as he trails it lower. My back arches, pushing my breasts right in front of his mouth. His lips close around one of my nipples. "Oh, God, yes, don't stop!" My movements are crazed. I'm so close to coming, and just when I reach the precipice—that enigmatic point of no return—Theo pulls away.

I go to protest. I want to say the words, but nothing comes out. I'm too far gone. Then he lifts my hips, lines his cock up with my entrance, and slams into me. And I explode. "I want you coming on my cock. I want your juices flooding me." He bites down on my shoulder.

"Yes! Yes!" I scream out.

He continues to grab my waist and slam me back down, moving me like I weigh nothing. Like I'm his own personal doll to do with as he pleases—which, in a way, I guess I am because I could never say no to him. Not when I know the kind of pleasure this man can bring me.

"Fuck!" he growls. My name leaves his lips in a whisper, his cock hardens, and his movements stiffen as he comes inside me, giving me every part of himself. I collapse on top of his chest, my body limp and spent.

His hands trail up and down my back before running through my hair. He does this a lot. Either he has a hair fetish, or he knows how much I love the sensation of his fingers combing through it. Even when he's angry, or upset, or maybe just frustrated with me (because he's definitely still *something*) he has a way of making me feel cherished and protected.

After a few minutes of basking in the afterglow, T stands me on my feet, picks up my dress, and tugs it over my head. Then he looks me up and down. "Go put something on that covers up all that skin, and I'll take you to see your dad." I open my mouth, to remind him that I can wear whatever I want, when he puts a finger to my lips. "Don't argue, Holly. You are not going to a place full of degenerates and showing off what belongs to me."

"I wasn't going to argue." I pivot towards the door, before stopping and turning back to him. "What exactly did I do to piss you off so much this morning?" I ask, because I can tell he's still boiling beneath the surface.

"I'm gonna go have Neo put another stitch in my shoulder. You should get dressed if you want to see your father." He leaves without so much as a glance in my direction.

And I'm left standing there, wondering what the hell just happened. Theo has never dismissed me like that before. I have no idea what's eating at him, and as much as I want to say *screw him and his brooding*, all I really want to do is fix it. Whatever is wrong, I want to make it right. I don't like the tension building between us. I don't chase after him though. Instead, I take a shower and get ready to see my father for the first time in over twelve months.

I should be more excited about the visit, but a part of me is still angry at him for doing what he did and leaving us. But there's that little girl part of me who just wants her daddy back. Before he went to jail, he was my rock. I could talk to him about anything, and he never judged me. And all I've done the past five years is *judge him* for his actions—resent him for them. How much of a hypocrite does that make me now? I'm married to one of New York's most ruthless crime bosses. Or so I'm told. I've yet to witness Theo be anything other than the sweet, protective man, who whispers promises of forever in my ear. Well, aside from this morning. I've been racking my brain, trying to figure out what I did to elicit such a harsh reaction. If he's not going to be mature about it and tell me, then I won't bother asking again.

I go downstairs in search of my husband, finding him and Neo in the midst of a heated conversation in the home office. Both men stop talking and look my way when I enter the room. I wring my hands in the fabric clinging to my abdomen. I chose a maxi dress. It falls down to my ankles, concealing *all that skin* that Theo seems to think needs covering. "Ah, I can come back, or I can call Reilly and see if she wants to go with me?" I offer.

T sighs, shaking his head. He still looks pissed as hell, but I don't feel like it's directed at me anymore. "No, dolcezza, I'll take you. Let's go." He picks up his wallet and keys from his desk. I don't know where he went to shower and change, but he's now dressed in a freshly pressed navy suit. His hair is still damp, and he smells clean and minty. How is it that I just had him less than an hour ago, and I already want nothing more than to kick Neo out of this office and have T fuck me over his desk?

I look to the desk, with that image in my head, and I can feel the blush creep up my face.

"Holly, are you okay?" T's voice is quiet as he steps in front of me.

"Ah, yeah. I'm fine," I croak out.

"Mmhmm, care to share what you were thinking about just now?"

"Nope, some thoughts should never leave my head."

T laughs before placing a hand on my lower back. "Neo, make the arrangements," he throws over his shoulder as he guides me out of the office.

Chapter Twenty-Two

Holly is sitting in the passenger seat chewing her fingernails. She's nervous. I can't tell if she's worried about seeing her father, or if it's because she knows I'm still pissed as hell. No matter how frustrated I am at her, I can't help but want to ease her worries. I reach over, grab one of her hands, and squeeze. "What's wrong?"

Her head turns towards me sharply, her green eyes

shooting daggers directly at mine. "Seriously? What's wrong? Nothing's wrong, Theo. What could possibly be wrong? I'm about to visit my father for the first time, in I don't even know how long. *In jail!* Oh, and there's the fact I'm taking my mafia boss husband—who, mind you, currently has a stick up his ass—to meet my father. *In jail!* Gee, Theo, I don't know what could possibly be wrong." She snatches her hand away.

"There is so much to unpack there, dolcezza, but let's start with the fact that I don't have a fucking stick up my ass."

"Oh, my bad. I thought your grumpy-ass mood was from the stick."

"I'm not grumpy. Just pissed off a little." Holly raises an eyebrow at me. "Okay, I'm fucking fuming. But I don't have a stick up anywhere."

"Care to share with the rest of the class why you're so *pissed off* then?"

I look at her, contemplating whether I should tell her the truth or not. In the end, I decide what the hell? Maybe it will prevent her from making the same mistake twice. "You called another man and asked for a fucking jet, Holly. You sought help from *another man*. Of course I'm fucking pissed off at that." Her eyebrows scrunch together, right before she bursts out laughing. "It's not fucking funny. You don't ever need to go to another man. *For anything.* You're my fucking wife. Anything you need, I can fucking give you, with a goddamn cherry on top too."

"Except you weren't going to give it to me, were you? I asked, and you said no."

"Because I want you safe. I don't want anything to happen to you," I huff. "I don't like fighting with you, Holly. It makes me sick to my stomach."

"This isn't fighting, T. This is you being an over-bearing alpha-ass."

"A what? Actually, it doesn't matter. Just... if you need anything, ask me. Don't ever call another man for anything again, and don't disrespect me in front of my men. It's not a good look."

"I didn't disrespect you, Theo. I would never do that."

I pick up her hand and bring it to my mouth, kissing it gently. "You might not have done so intentionally, dolcezza. But what you did, calling on another man for help, that's a huge disrespect to your husband, especially in our world."

"I'm sorry you felt that way. It wasn't my intention. I promise. I freaked out. I didn't want to be separated from you again, and I was prepared to do whatever I had to, in order to follow you to Italy. If you need to be somewhere, then so do I."

"Okay. If I survive this visit with your father, I promise I will never leave you again, unless I have absolutely no choice."

"Why wouldn't you survive?"

"I married the man's daughter, without asking his permission. And now I'm stealing that daughter to live with me in my fucked-up, dangerous underworld, all the way in New York. You really think your father's not gonna wanna kill me?" I smile at her.

She doesn't return it. "That's not funny. I don't like thinking of my father as a killer. But that's what he is, isn't he?"

I glance over at her; her eyes are glassy. "Holly, your father didn't do anything I wouldn't have done myself. Anything I haven't already done myself. And you don't look at me any differently, even knowing what I'm capable of. You shouldn't look at him any differently either. You don't know what you're capable of doing for your children, for someone you love, until you're in that position yourself."

"It's not what he did. It's the fact that he left us. We needed him, and he left."

"You can't hold on to that resentment. It's not good for anyone. Try to forgive him, Holly." I can't fathom what she went through when her father was sent away. I've seen plenty of men get sentenced to hard time, but no one I really gave a damn about. Of course, the Feds are always waiting for one of us to fuck up, so they can stick us with some bullshit charges. But I don't plan on ever being stupid enough to let that happen. I wonder if Holly would resent me if it did though? Would I expect her to wait around for me, like the other wives in the family? I'm not sure. What I am sure of is the fact that I'd slaughter any fucker she tried to move on with, anyone who thought they could touch what's mine. I'd make certain the whole fucking world got *that* message and knew exactly who she belonged to.

I pull into the parking lot at the prison. It's a shitty-looking building with an unkempt landscape. I always get chills whenever I walk into these places. I check my phone to see if Neo was able to make the arrangements for today.

Neo: All set, boss.

Me: Thanks. Have the jet ready to leave tonight at six.

Neo: What about your mum?

Shit, I forgot about her. I can't leave her behind when I'm taking every man we have for Holly's protection.

Me: Tell her to pack lightly.

Neo: I'll just tell her to pack. I don't have a death wish, boss.

I roll my eyes. My mother wouldn't know how to pack lightly if her life depended on it.

"T, you don't have to come in with me, you know. I get it if you don't want to."

"Dolcezza, under no circumstances would I ever let you walk into that building alone. Come on. Let's do this." Holly's palm grips mine tightly as I lead her into the reception area.

"Name?" Some burley guy sitting behind the counter spits out the question, without even looking up from the phone in his hand.

"Ah, Holly Reynolds. Here to see Steven Reynolds." I pause at Holly's use of her maiden name. What the fuck is she doing? The guard looks up at her, his eyes roaming over her chest. My body's pulsating with the need to gouge his fucking eyes out.

"You'll have to step into that room for a search." He nods his head to the side, and Holly stiffens behind me.

"Like fuck she will. Any of you filthy motherfuckers even think about touching my wife, and I'll cut your damn fingers off and shove them up your asses," I growl. Who the fuck does this prick think he is, telling Holly she needs to be searched? "Let's try this again. Theo and Holly Valentino, here to see Steven Reynolds." I smirk as the guard pales and his eyes widen.

Yeah, that's what I thought, fucker.

Chapter Twenty-Three

Holly

I can feel Theo's body vibrating with anger; the heat radiating off him is palpable. I glance from him to the guard, who now looks like he's seen a ghost. Oh my God, what was I thinking? I shouldn't have brought T here. He's a bloody criminal. And not just any criminal. No, he's the head criminal—the boss! "Ah, sure, straight through that door, sir. Your appointment is ready." The guard swallows loudly and points behind us.

I turn to follow the man's directions. However, Theo is a brick wall. Unyielding. His dark gaze is locked on the guard's. "T, come on. It's okay." I try to force him to look at me, to move, so we can get this visit over with and leave. But he doesn't budge. "Theo, let's go!" He looks down at me, his lips twitching. Yep, I'm sure he's trying not to laugh at the fact I just pulled out my well-practiced *teacher voice* on him.

"Sure thing." He drapes an arm over my shoulder, kissing my forehead as we walk towards the open door. As soon as I step into the room, I can't stop the tears from streaming down my cheeks. I run, freezing just short of my father. I want nothing more than to wrap myself around him and have him hold me. But that's not allowed. I don't want to cause any trouble, so I stand in front of where he sits. The door clicks loudly behind me, but I don't move. Not until T comes up next to me and leans down to whisper in my ear. "You can hug your father, Holly. No one's gonna stop you."

I look over to him and then around the room. The guard left. They just left us in here. That's never happened before. I want to question it, but I honestly don't care what strings T had to pull to make this happen. "Dad, I've missed you so much. I'm sorry." I throw myself at my father as he stands to catch me.

Being in his arms feels like home. "Shh, Hol. It's

okay, sweetheart. It's okay." He holds me tighter, neither one of us wanting to let go. After a few minutes, my dad pulls back and kisses me on the forehead. "I'm glad you're here. You look good." He runs his eyes up and down my smaller frame. I'm not sure what he's searching for, but he does this every time I see him.

"Thanks. You do too."

"Come on. Sit down. Tell me everything. What's been happening?" My dad glances from Theo to me, the questions written all over his face. I lower myself to the chair, and Theo sits next to me. He's silent. He hasn't said a word yet. He does, however, put his hand on my thigh and squeeze.

"Ah, well, I kind of... I got married. This is Theo. My husband," I say quickly.

My dad looks between us before he offers a sad smile. "I wish I could have been there. I'm sorry I missed it." He drops his eyes to his hands, now resting on the table.

"Oh, don't worry! We're having a real big wedding in a few months. You'll be able to make it and walk me down the aisle. Right? You're getting out in a couple of days."

"Why are you having another wedding?" my dad asks.

I'm not sure how to answer that. I can't really say that it's because we only signed papers, in order to avoid a huge shit fight with a mob boss of another family—oh, and my husband's previously arranged marriage. Theo saves me from having to respond. "That's my fault, sir. Sorry, though it's a pleasure to finally meet you. You see, I couldn't wait to make Holly my wife. We eloped, but we are planning a big ceremony when everyone can be there. I do apologize for not asking you for your daughter's hand in marriage first." *And cue the swoon moment.* He always knows the right thing to say.

"Something tells me it wouldn't have really mattered if I had said no."

I gasp. "Dad!" I've never heard my dad speak like this—he was rough, firm, *different*.

"It's okay, dolcezza," Theo says, smiling at me. Then he looks directly at my father. "With all due respect, sir, no, your blessing would not have made a difference to me, but I'm sure it would have meant the world to Holly."

My dad smiles. "Good, the last thing I need is for my daughter to be stuck with a fool missing his backbone." Okay, I knew my dad would have changed. I mean, how can someone spend five years in prison and *not* be affected. But this man in front of me is completely different. My dad never would have said something like that before. I don't even know how to respond.

An hour later, we exit the building. This is the part I've always hated the most: walking out and leaving my dad stuck behind those walls. I can't imagine what he's been through over the years. "Your dad looks good," Theo says as he starts the car.

"Yeah."

"Dolcezza, three more days, and he's out of there. And you won't ever have to come back to a place like this."

"You can't promise me that, T. Anything could happen in the future. We need to live for today, make the most of what we have now." It saddens me to think that I could one day be visiting my husband in a place just like this. I'm not even sure how he's managed to avoid ending up behind bars for so long. "How do you do it?" I ask him.

"Do what?"

"How do you get everyone to do your bidding? Wherever you go, people seem to know who you are, and they don't ever question anything you do. You got my dad an early release, just like that." I click my fingers together.

"It wasn't *just like that*, dolcezza. I paid off the

right people. That's all. It's about knowing who to go to when you need to get shit done."

I spin his words over in my head. He had to pay people off? Who? And how much? "Theo, how much did you have to pay to get my dad out?"

"Not as much as I was prepared to. I'd do anything for you, Holly."

"I know that. But I'm curious. How much?"

T sighs. "Five hundred thousand."

Five hundred thousand? That's all it took? Reilly and I could have paid that if we knew the right people. "I can pay you back," I say.

"You're not fucking paying me back. Besides, my money is your money, Holly. So, really, I used your money to pay it anyway." He smirks.

"That means my money is your money too. And it won't matter if I transfer the remainder of my trust into your account." I think I've managed to outsmart him. But I should know he's always one step ahead.

"You could try. But it won't work. Your money is your money, Holly. You're not transferring it anywhere. Besides, I had my bank block any transfers from your account into mine, back when we first met and you were insisting on paying me for a fucking coffee."

"How? What?" How does he do this?

"Dolcezza, I'm not fighting with you over money."

"We're not fighting, Theo. We are having a conversation."

"We're leaving at six tonight. Is there anything else you want to do before we fly out?" I chew on my lip and stare at him. There's a lot I want to do with him, *to him*. Theo notices me eyeing him up. He laughs. "Unless you want me to pull this car over and fuck you right here, you need to stop looking at me like I'm your next meal."

"As much as I want you to do just that, I think I should go and see my sister and mum before we leave. You don't have to come with me if you have other things to do."

He turns to me and shakes his head. "The only thing I have to do today is you, dolcezza." He smirks. "So, where to first?"

"Reilly's house." I take out my phone and send her a text.

Me: I'm on my way to your house with T.

Reilly: Right now? Shit, okay.

Me: Can you get Mum to meet us at yours? I'm going to Italy with T tonight.

My phone rings in my hand, but I don't answer it, pressing decline instead before tucking it back into my bag and ignoring the onslaught of messages I know my sister will be sending in response.

Five minutes later, T's phone rings through the car's audio system. "Hello," he answers.

"Theo, what the hell are you doing, taking my sister

to Italy? Are you nuts? Anything could happen to her there. I don't know what shady shit you're up to, but I sure as hell won't let you involve my sister in whatever it is."

I'm speechless. I knew Reilly had no sense of self-preservation or anything, but to flat-out go off on Theo? She clearly has no filter or fear either. "Reilly, stop..." I'm interrupted by Theo.

"Mrs. Williamson, I understand your concerns regarding my wife. And because you are family, I will allow you certain concessions others are not privy to. But do not, and I repeat: Do. Not. Ever. Think you can tell me what to do with my wife." Oh, he's not impressed. I don't blame him. If someone tried to tell me I couldn't take Theo somewhere, I wouldn't respond kindly either.

"She's not just my sister; she's my twin. That's like way more than just a sister. If anything happens to her, I will find you, and no amount of beefcake goons will be able to save your ass from my wrath."

"Reilly, that's enough. You're overreacting, and you two need to stop talking about me like I'm not here. Theo is not willingly taking me to Italy. I forced his hand. So you can stop blaming him. You will be nice when we get to your place, or I'll just leave."

"Ah, sure. Okay, well, I guess I'll see you soon." Reilly hangs up.

I look over to Theo and see a huge grin on his face. "What are you smiling about?" I ask, confused.

"You are *stupefacente*, but I don't need you to come to my defense, Holly."

"Did you just call me stupid?" I try to repeat the word in my head: *stupefacente*. I can't think of anything else it could mean.

"No, I said you are *amazing*. Dolcezza, you are the furthest thing from stupid."

"Mhm, sure," I mumble, making a mental note to Google that word later.

We park in front of Reilly and Bray's house. I remember picking Reilly up from this street the first time she stayed the night. I never thought she'd end up living here. To be honest, I never thought she'd get married at all. "Nice neighborhood," Theo says, looking around.

"Bray wants a soccer team of kids. He bought this house, ready for that future before he even met my sister."

Theo kills the engine and turns my way, his gaze searing through me. "What about you? Do you want a soccer team?"

I can't help but laugh. I'm a teacher. I love kids by nature, but I don't want a heap of my own. "I want one, maybe two. But no more than that. How about you?" I throw the question back.

"I want as many as you'll give me. I want a bunch of little Hollys running around." His answer surprises me. I'm not sure why, but I never pictured Theo as a kid person. "You want daughters? You know daughters grow up to bring boys home—boys like you." I smile.

Theo shrugs. "I can think of thirty different ways to make a man disappear without even trying. I'm sure I can manage to scare off any stronzi stupid enough to come around our daughters."

"Stronzi?" I ask.

"Fuckers." He grins as he gets out of the car. My stomach twists with nerves. I have to introduce Theo to my mum. What if she doesn't like him? I'm still trying to wrap my head around my dad's reaction, which I was not expecting at all. "What's wrong?" T lifts my chin until my eyes meet his.

"I'm nervous. You're about to meet my mum, T. She wasn't exactly thrilled I went and got married."

"Don't worry about it. Ladies love me, Holly. Your mother will too." He offers me that panty-melting smile, and I roll my eyes.

I lead Theo up to the house and walk in. Following the noise, I find my mum and Reilly in the kitchen arguing over baked goods, as Bray fills his mouth with brownies. I grab for the tray, but my hand gets slapped away before I can even touch one. "Hey."

"Those are not for you, Holly," my mum says, holding the metal pan just out of reach.

I glance between Reilly and Bray. My sister looks utterly pissed, while her husband's sporting a smug grin. "What the hell?"

"She made them for me, Holls, sorry. I'd share, but

you know... too good." Bray laughs as he pops another piece into his mouth.

"Actually, I made them for Theo. You're just lucky you got one first." My mum pivots, holding the tray out to us. "Hi, I'm Lynne. Here, these are for you."

"Ah, thanks. It's a pleasure to meet you, ma'am." Theo accepts her offering, raising a square to his lips, but before he takes a bite, he holds it to my mouth instead. I don't hesitate to chew half the brownie off. He arches a brow but doesn't say anything.

"Ah, why? Why can't you share with me like that, Bray?" Reilly squeals.

"Well, he's only sharing because he hasn't tasted them yet. Wait until he realizes how good they are." Bray laughs again.

I watch Theo close his eyes as he sinks his teeth into my mum's brownie. *Yep, they are that bloody amazing.* "Mmm, wow." Theo takes another one off the platter. I wait, wondering if he'll still share with me, or if they really are just that good. "There is nothing I wouldn't give up for you, dolcezza," Theo says as he breaks the brownie in half before handing me a piece.

"Way to make me look bad, bro," Bray pouts.

"Shut up and watch, Bray. Maybe you should take down some notes. Theo, you could give him lessons, right?" Reilly asks.

"Mum, we went and saw Dad this morning. He looks good; he's excited to come home." I change the topic.

"Wait, you both went? And you're still standing?"

"Reilly, shut up. Dad happened to love Theo—a little too much actually. It was weird."

"Yeah, he likes this one too." Reilly points her thumb at Bray.

"Okay, coffee! Who wants coffee?" Mum spins towards the kitchen. She's avoiding the conversation. I let it drop, deciding not to put a damper on our time together.

Chapter Twenty-Four

"**W**ould you stop fidgeting already. You're making me fucking nervous," Neo whispers to me in Italian.

"I can't help it. You know I was fucking ambushed on my way out of the country. God only knows what the fuck we're about to walk into when we land. Except, *this time*, I have my fucking mother and wife to worry about." I sigh. I can't believe I let Holly weasel her way into coming with me. I should have put my foot down more firmly and insisted she stayed in fucking Sydney. But selfishly I let her accompany me, because I didn't want to be without her. What if that same selfishness gets her fucking killed? I can't live without her. I *won't* live without her.

"Do you really think we're walking into trouble?" Neo asks.

"I don't know," I answer honestly. Because I really don't fucking know what to expect, and it's eating me up. My nerves are fucking frayed, and I've never been more on edge. If it was just us—me and my men—yeah, I'd be worried but I wouldn't be *this* fucking worried.

The fact that Holly's with me, that's what has me crawling out of my skin. I know it's my fault. I let her come... Then again, there really is no *letting* Holly do anything. A character trait I both admire and despise equally. Sometimes I think my life would be so much easier if she was a little wallflower, who would listen and follow my every command. On the other hand, I know I'd be bored shitless without her spunk and determination.

"You've made the appropriate arrangements for the estate?" I ask Neo. I'm pretty sure word has spread that I'm very much alive and not actually dead. And so, I have no intention of staying away from the family compound now. I haven't heard a peep out of the other three, which is fucking strange, to say the least. Whatever the fuck they're up to, I need to find out and make sure I'm one step ahead.

"Yeah, we're all set. I've got three cars meeting us at the airfield." Neo's voice breaks through my thoughts.

"Good." I nod. Then I stand and head towards the back of the jet, where Holly is sleeping.

"Theo, sit down for a minute." My mother stops me on the way.

"Ma, how you holdin' up?" I haven't really had time for her lately, and I feel like a shitty son for what I've put her through.

"I'm fine. Don't worry about me. How are *you*? It's a lot: taking over, running the family, doing it all so suddenly. I don't want the stress to eat at you. You were a born leader, Theo."

"Thanks, Ma, but I'm fine."

"You're not, but I also know you're not going to talk to me about whatever it is that's worrying you. You should talk to someone though."

"I'm fine, Ma," I repeat.

"I really like Holly. You did good choosing her. I'm sorry it took me a while to come around to the idea."

I'm speechless. I knew my mother had grown fond of Holly, but I never expected to hear an apology. "Thanks. She's something else. I don't deserve her, but I'm sure as hell glad I have her."

"You deserve everything, Theo. You're a good person." My mother leans forward and kisses both of my cheeks.

"Thanks, Ma." I know I'm not a good person, but I'm not going to argue with my mother about that. I won't win. "I'm gonna go check on Holly. We should be landing in about thirty." I continue towards the bedroom. Holly tried to make my mother lie down when we first boarded, but Ma wouldn't hear of it. She hates flights, and she especially hates sleeping on flights—something about how she *doesn't want to miss when the plane goes down.* Though, if you were to ask me, sleeping through your impending death seems like a good way to go.

I push the door open, closing it gently behind me. I know we only have thirty minutes until we land, but there's a lot that can be done in thirty minutes. I haven't had the pleasure of giving Holly her membership to the Mile High Club yet, and there's no better time than the present.

I pull my shirt over my head, then toe off my shoes and socks. I'm left in just my sweats. Holly doesn't stir, as I carefully pull the blankets away from her and gently roll her so she's lying flat on her back, before settling myself between her legs. Lifting her dress, I'm pleasantly surprised to find she's not wearing underwear. I smirk, recalling the numerous pairs I've destroyed in my haste to get at her pussy. It's my favorite fucking drug: intoxicating, suffocating, and all-consuming in the most delicious of ways. My mouth waters as I look down at her opening. It's slightly glistening with wetness, and I wish more than anything that I could jump into her dreams and know what she's picturing right now.

My tongue slowly slides between her folds, and her hips lift off the bed in response. I keep my eyes trained on her face. She's still asleep, but she's beginning to stir. I twirl my tongue around her clit, savoring her taste. "Mmm, don't stop," her raspy, sleep-laden voice whispers out.

"I don't ever plan to, dolcezza."

I watch as her eyes pop open in surprise. "T?" she questions as she looks around the room. I go back to work, licking, biting, and sucking on her pussy. "Just so there's no misunderstanding, I'm okay with this method of waking up, for future reference." She smiles down at me as her hands tangle in my hair.

"I promise to wake you just like this as often as I possibly can, dolcezza." I insert one finger into her opening, pumping back and forth a few times before adding another. Her walls tighten around the intrusion. I bite down and suck on her clit, while my two fingers are sliding in and out of her pussy as my thumb pushes against her ass. It doesn't take long before she's coming all over me. Her hands hold my face to her as she shamelessly grinds into my mouth. Once she's coming down, her grip on my hair loosens.

I climb to my knees and pull my sweats down, freeing my raging cock. Then, lining myself up with Holly's entrance, I thrust forward and her head rolls back. I pick up her hips, lifting them off the bed, and her legs wrap around my waist like a vise. "Oh, God, T. Yes!" she screams.

"Shh." I cover her mouth with my palm. "Do you want me to continue, dolcezza?" I ask. She nods. "Then you need to be quiet. I don't want every other fucker on this aircraft to know what you sound like when you're coming apart for me. Those sounds are mine, Holly. All of you is mine. Every. Fucking. Inch." Keeping my hand in place to muffle her cries of pleasure, I fuck her hard and fast. "This is going to be quick. We're landing soon."

Holly's hand finds its way to my balls, and she starts rolling them around in her fingers. The tingles crawl up my spine, and my every nerve ending clenches as she milks the orgasm from me. Moments later, I'm emptying everything I have inside her. I'll never tire of fucking her raw, nothing between us but skin and perspiration. I collapse on the bed, pulling her into me.

"When all this shit is settled, and we're back in New York, I want you to stop taking the pill," I whisper against her hair. I shock myself with the admission, but I think I shock Holly even more. Her whole body stills, before she untangles herself from my arms and pops up.

"We only just got married, Theo. We only just met... Do you really think we're ready to have babies?" Her face pales a little.

"It doesn't have to be tomorrow. Or even next year.

Stop worrying. If you're not ready, then we'll wait." I sit up and pull her over my lap so she's straddling me.

"Okay... I'm sorry. I do want to have kids. I just don't know if I'm ready to share you with anyone else yet. I already have to share you with so many people."

"Holly, nobody is more important to me than you. No matter how busy I get, or how much craziness happens in my world, you are—and always will be—my number one priority." I mean every word of it. No one comes before my wife. Ever. But my promises don't comfort her. If anything, they make her angry.

Her face reddens as she jumps off the bed. Pulling her dress down and running her hands over the fabric, in an attempt to smooth out the wrinkles, she turns around with her hands on her hips and stares daggers in my direction. I try hard to fight the smile that wants to grace my lips. She's fucking gorgeous when she's mad. "I'm the most important thing, huh? Tell me, T, how important was I when you let me think you were dead? How important was I when you and Neo concocted that stupid plan? When you forced me to watch that house explode, all while thinking you were inside?" She raises her eyebrows to further express her point.

I thought we had moved past this. But clearly, she's still festering some negative emotions towards that whole ordeal. "Dolcezza, it's because of you that I did what I had to do. I needed to fix the situation in New York. I need to make it safe for you to live there. I can't have shit happening in my city that will put you at risk."

"You know what? It doesn't even matter. I know who you are, Theo. I know you have to do things I don't like. But for some reason, I can't seem to imagine a life without you. I don't want to know what a life without you is anymore. I'm still bloody pissed about what you did, and I will be for a while, but above that, I'm bloody relieved that I still get to have you."

"You won't have to live without me, Holly. Before you know it, I'll have this shit sorted out, and we can all go home. You can return to your job and teach those spoiled little brats at that stuck-up school." Holly winces and averts her eyes. "What? You don't want to go back to New York?"

"Of course I do. I loved it for the whole few weeks I got to spend there. However, I do need to find a new job. I kind of... well, I... I got fired," she huffs out.

I'm speechless. "How could you have possibly been fired? You were only there for a day. And Neo had an agreement with the principal; your job should be waiting for you," I ask, confused.

"Well, that's the thing... schools tend to like their teachers to, you know, turn up and teach the kids. I know Neo said he had it sorted, but obviously things change." She shrugs and tries to play it off like it's not a big deal.

I saw how much effort she put into planning and preparing for her new class. I know how much she loves her job. "Why didn't you say something? When did this even happen?" I pull my phone out and scroll through the list of numbers, trying to find a contact, someone, anyone I know who can get her reinstated.

"I didn't want to bring it up. You've been really busy, and I don't want to waste what little time we have together. It's okay. I'm sure I can find something, or I can do temp work for a while. I have my trust, so it's not like I'm desperate for the paycheck. I just can't actually live in the States without a job. I'm there on a work permit, T. I've already told you this."

She has her trust. "Dolcezza, fuck *your* trust. You have the fucking Valentino last name and the bank account that comes with it. You don't need to work another day in your life if you choose not to. Oh, and in case you forgot, we're married, so you don't need a fucking visa either. Let some asshole try to tell my wife she can't live wherever the fuck she wants to live—I dare him."

Holly rolls her eyes at me. "We should probably take our seats. You said we were landing soon, right?"

I look at the time on my phone. "Yeah, we are. They're probably circling, waiting for us." I know my pilots are pedantic with safety. I fucking pay them to be. They're not going to land without everyone in a belted seat. "That school is the one missing out by not keeping you. You are an amazing teacher, Holly. You're the smartest, kindest person I know. It's their loss, not yours." I kiss her forehead as we sit down.

Then I take Holly's hand, dropping the subject. *For now*.

Exiting the plane, I see the three cars Neo said would be here, but I also see a chopper waiting not far down the runway and fucking Donatello making his way towards us. I lean into Holly and whisper, "He's an important man, dolcezza. The Don of Dons. Whatever you do, do not point a gun at his head." I smirk.

"It was one time, T. Really? Am I never going to live that down?" Holly hisses.

"Theo, welcome back." Donatello holds out a palm.

I shake it and introduce Holly. "This is Holly, my wife."

Donatello schools his surprise, before leaning in and kissing her cheeks. "Benvenuto in famiglia, Holly. Lovely to meet you." I don't have time to ponder why he's *welcoming* my wife *to the family*. Perhaps it's an old school Italian thing. "Gloria, più bella che mai." He steps towards my mother to greet her.

I was already aware they knew each other. Apparently, my mother was friends with his sister (or so I've been told) and they have mingled in the same crowds over the years at events. But watching the way my mother stiffens at Donatello's presence, paired with her wary eyes, which travel to me then back to the man in front of her, has me wondering just how *well*.

"Donatello, I wasn't expecting to see you here," my mother says.

"Well, it's not every day that I get to see an old friend on the mainland, Gloria." Donatello looks towards the three cars lining the tarmac before nodding his head at me. "Theo, a word, if you wouldn't mind." He turns and walks a few steps away from our group.

"Stay with her," I say to Neo as I follow. He goes to open his mouth to argue, but I don't wait for him to get a word out. "You know, if you wanted to chitchat, simply picking up the phone works wonders these days." I smirk at Donatella.

"How's the shoulder?"

"I've had worse." I shrug the limb in question. It still fucking hurts like a motherfucker. I'm just not about to announce that to everyone.

"I thought I'd offer you a ride to the estate. I've had rooms made up in my home for you and your guests."

"Why?" I tilt my head. Why would he want us to stay with him?

"T, you were ambushed on your way out of the country two days ago. Do you really think you should be out driving around?"

"I'm sure my men are just as good, if not better, than yours."

"And you're prepared to risk the safety and well-being of your new bride? For what? Your pride? Over not wanting to accept the aid I'm offering? Something very few people ever get from me, I might add."

"Again, why? Why are you trying to help me?"

"We have common interests. Plus, your mother and I are old friends. There's enough room on the chopper for you and three others. The rest can follow my men to the compound." Donatello turns and walks away.

I nod my head to Neo, and he jogs forward. We walk back, side-by-side, my eyes firmly trained on Holly as I relay the new lodging plan. To say he's pissed and apprehensive as fuck about the idea would be an understatement. But Donatello is right. I'd rather not put Holly (or my mother) at any unnecessary risk. "Dolcezza, ever been in a helicopter?" I ask, wrapping my arms around her.

"Nope."

"Great, another one of your firsts I'll have the plea-sure of taking. Come on, we're getting a ride with Donatello."

"Are you sure that's wise, Theo? We should go back to our estate," my mother interjects.

"Ma, Donatello has opened his home to us. It would be rude, and extremely stupid, to refuse such a *generous* offer," I say between clenched teeth. Why the hell is she suddenly questioning everything? She never used to question my father. Whatever he said was law, and you either followed suit, or you ended up in a shallow grave somewhere.

"Come on, we're all just tired from the flight. Gloria, sit with me. You can point out all the landmarks as we fly over them." Holly links her arm through my mother's and waits for me to lead the way, while Neo walks off to update the rest of the men before joining us again.

"Wait, Sonnie isn't coming?" Holly asks, watching him climb into one of the SUVs.

"No, he's not," I grumble. She is getting way too close to the fucking men who are supposed to be protecting her. They can't do their job properly if they're too busy being friendly with my fucking wife.

Chapter Twenty-Five

Holly

I feel like I'm in a dream, an amazing dream that I never want to wake up from. I'm literally flying over Italy in a helicopter. I can't keep the smile from my lips as I watch the city and landscapes below us.

I grab T's face in my hands and slam my mouth to his. "I love this. Oh my God, T, I can't believe I'm flying over Italy. It's stunning. Why didn't you tell me it's so beautiful? I mean, of course I knew it would be. But, wow. Just... wow. Look at this." I point out the window.

I hear Neo's chuckle over my headset, and that's when I realize that everyone can hear my ramblings, not just Theo. I can feel my cheeks heating up.

"We are blessed with a beautiful country, bella. You should make sure to see as much as you can while you're here," Donatello says.

I smile politely at the older man. There's something so familiar about him. The more I look, the more I see his resemblance to Theo. It's his eyes; they're the same. "How are you two related? Cousins, uncle?" I ask T, pointing between him and Donatello. Gloria chokes on the water she was drinking, while Donatello is quick to help her, rubbing his hands along her back.

"We're not related, dolcezza. Donatello is the head of a different family." Theo kisses my temple. I love that he never cares who is around us. He always finds a way to touch me, little kisses here and there. He's not afraid to show anyone that I'm his. I'd be lying if I said I hated it.

"Oh, okay. You just look similar—that's all." I shrug it off and continue staring out the window.

I'm exhausted. This jet lag has thrown me. All I want to do is curl up and sleep for the next two days. I'm just stepping out of the shower, a shower I'll be making use of as often as possible before I have to leave here. It was pure heaven. I wrap a towel around me and walk into our guest bedroom. It's more like a mini apartment: it has a bar, a kitchenette, and its own plunge pool on the balcony. Who needs a resort when you have friends with houses like this? I should care that the foundation of all these amenities was forged out of violence and blood money, but I can't bring myself to think on it now.

The door to the room is ajar. I walk over to close it before I get changed but stop at the threshold. "I need you to go to this address and get Lana out of the country. Send her ass home." Theo's voice is quiet but maintains that harsh undertone.

"What the fuck is she even doing here, T?" Neo counters. Good bloody question—a question I'd very much like answered right now too. That, and why T didn't tell me she was here.

"Her and her Russian fucking boytoy hijacked my flight. Look, they're both staying at this cottage. Just tell them to leave. We need clear heads if we're gonna get this done tonight. The auction starts in two hours. We should get moving."

"Okay, I'll handle Lana, but you are not going to that fucking auction alone. I'm coming."

I really shouldn't be eavesdropping; this is not the

sort of stuff I need to hear. But, at the same time, I can't *not* hear it either.

"No, I need you to stay here with Holly, Neo. I can't do this *and* be worried about her. I need to know she's safe"

"She's locked up in Donatello's fortress. Nothing's going to happen to her inside the compound. Let Sonnie stay with her. I'm coming with you," Neo demands. I don't think I've ever heard him speak so forcefully before.

"Fucking hell, fine, but I want more than just Sonnie. I don't trust any of the fuckers around here. At least four men at the door to this room. Have them stationed there in ten. We need to head out. And make the arrangements to get Lana out of the goddamn country before she gets herself killed." T steps through the door, and I freeze. I've been caught red-handed, listening in on a conversation I'm not meant to know anything about. I swallow, my nerves running rampant, and hold the towel tighter to my chest. "Fanculo, how much of that did you hear, dolcezza?" T tilts his head to the side, his eyes roaming up and down my body.

"I-I didn't mean to. I'm sorry," I stammer out.

"You sure about that? Because from where I'm standing, it looked completely intentional."

"Why didn't you mention that Lana came to Italy with you?" I ask, turning the questions back on him instead.

"That's what you're concerned about? Fine, I didn't tell you because it didn't seem important."

"You took another woman across the globe, and you didn't think that was important?"

"It's not like that, and you know it, Holly. Or did you miss the part about her bringing her fucking Russian boyfriend in tow?"

"Nope." Call me a fool, but I trust Theo more than I've ever trusted anyone. I know there is nothing between him and Lana, but I don't feel like letting him off the hook that easy.

"Do you really think that little of me, Holly? That I'd step out on you?" he asks, folding his arms over his chest. He tries to mask the hurt in his eyes, in his voice. But I see it, and it coaxes the guilt to the surface.

"No, I don't. I have no doubt that you are nothing but faithful, Theo. But that's not the point. The point is you're hiding shit from me. And I don't like it." He sighs in response, running his hands through his hair. He looks tired. Stressed. I'm not helping him at all right now. "You should stay in and sleep tonight. Whatever plans you have, I'm sure they can wait until morning."

"I want nothing more than to crawl into that bed with you and not leave it for at least a week. But I have a few things I need to take care of. Don't wait up for me, dolcezza. I don't know how long I'll be."

His hand tugs at my loose strands, tilting my face upwards. Then his lips descend onto mine, parting

227

them with a single swipe of his tongue. This kiss is hungry, passionate, driven. I feel every ounce of love, of desire and devotion, this man has for me. All in a single kiss. His hands tremble as he pulls away. "Please don't go. I don't have a good feeling about this, T. Please don't leave me again," I whisper selfishly. I know it's not a fair request. But right now, I don't care what's fair.

"I love you—never forget that. I love you so fucking much, Holly," he says, ignoring my plea. Then he walks out and closes the door.

Why do I have this dread in the pit of my stomach? I feel helpless, and all I can think to do is send up a prayer that T makes it back to me in one piece. I'm not going to be able to get any sleep tonight without a bit of extra help, no matter how exhausted my body is. I throw on Theo's discarded t-shirt, pour myself a huge glass of red wine, and sit on the bed. It's not long before I place the wine glass on the bedside table and hop under the covers. I can feel the sleep pulling me under. I try to fight it, but it's useless.

I wake with a start. What the hell was that? The room is dark, but a little light seeps in from the adjoining bathroom. I stand and shriek when I hear it again. It's the unmistakable sound of a gunshot. "Sonnie?" I call out. My heart stops as the door opens and Sonnie's body falls to the floor, blood pooling around his head. I hear the scream that leaves my lungs before I register that it's coming from me.

I'm staring at the older man standing in my doorway, his white shirt coated in red. He's aiming a gun in my direction as he walks towards me. I'm frozen to the spot. I can't move. "W-who are you?" I manage to ask, right before he reaches out and backhands me across my face. The blow sends me stumbling, and I land on the bed.

"Fucking whore, ya think you get to question me? That's not how this is going to work." He steps closer, and I'm repulsed by the putrid smell of alcohol on his breath as he leans in to me. "You can thank your husband for what's about to happen to you. He should have left things alone. He should have stayed out of my fucking business. Well, let's see how he likes it when I get in his."

He begins to unbutton his pants, and I know I need to act, to get away before something happens that I'll never be able to recover from. I kick out my legs, knocking the guy in the stomach, and make a run for the door. But I trip over Sonnie's body and land in a puddle of his blood.

I'm yanked backwards by my hair while I'm still trying to recover. "Bitch, I'm going to fucking enjoy this even more now. I'll film it too, make sure your stupid fucking husband doesn't miss a minute."

"No, don't touch me!" I yell, my fight finally taking the reins. I hit and kick everything I can make contact with. I will not let this motherfucker rape me and show it to Theo. That would fucking destroy us. Destroy *him*. I bite down on the man's arm, hard enough to draw blood, but that only earns me a punch to the temple. My vision blurs as the room spins, and I'm thrown down onto the bed. "No!" I call out again.

Get up, Holly. Get up and run! My internal voice is urging me forward. I just can't seem to get my limbs to comply. He pulls out a knife, and my body goes rigid. All I can think is: *Please don't let Theo see this. Please God, don't let this happen.* He runs the blade over my shirt and tears the fabric open, exposing my naked chest.

"No, fuck you!" I scream as I try to get myself free from beneath him. He reaches out and gropes at my breasts, his fingers roughly digging into my flesh. Then his hand travels down and palms my pussy. *Oh, God, this is it...* I look around, trying to find something, anything I can use as a weapon to get him off me. But his weight has me trapped in place. I feel his fingers push inside me and I scream out in pain, the agony and humiliation of the unwanted penetration comparable to being stabbed through the heart with a knife. "Stop! Please, stop!" I resort to begging.

I close my eyes, deciding it might be better if I don't

see this happening, if I imagine I'm somewhere else. I can pretend it's just a horrible nightmare, and soon I'll wake up and it'll all be over, except this is my greatest fear come true. But then... everything stops. The insurmountable weight is lifted from my body, and I open my eyes to a fuming Donatello holding a gun to the other man's head.

"Fucking thirty years, and this is how you repay me? You no good son of a bitch. That's my fucking daughter-in-law, you asshole. Did you really think you'd get away with touching her? I should fucking chain you up in the basement and let you await your fate from Theo. I hear he has techniques that'll make the things we've done look like fucking child's play." Donatello smiles. It's almost as if he's... *proud?*

But I don't have the time (or energy) to continue to decipher the man's facial expressions. I need to get out of here. I tug the remnants of my shirt back across my chest and stand. Just as I step off the bed, I see a discarded gun on the floor. I pick it up. My mind clears and I focus on one thing. One person. I aim the barrel at the asshole seething on the floor as he spews something out in Italian to Donatello. "I fucking said no!" I hiss, then pull the trigger. Three times. I watch as his body convulses with each impact of metal to flesh and red further darkens his white shirt. I don't lower my weapon though. Instead, I aim it at Donatello. I can't trust anyone in this house. "Where is my husband?" I ask him.

Donatello lowers his own gun, tucking it in the back of his waistband. He then raises his hands. "I'm not going to hurt you, bella."

"Where is Theo?"

"He's not here. Come on, let me get you out of this room. I'll take you to Gloria; she's down the hall. Just lower *that* and follow me," he says.

I don't move. I'm not following him anywhere. I have no idea if he was in on this whole thing or not. "Call Theo. Now. Tell him he needs to come back."

"Okay, I'll call him for you." I watch as he pulls a phone out of his pocket. But before he can dial, several men rush into the room with their weapons drawn, each of the barrels aimed in my direction. "Put your fucking guns down. You are not to hurt a fucking hair on that girl's head. She's famiglia." They do as they're told, lowering their sights, but none of them leave the room. Are they really afraid of what I might do to their boss?

I can hear the call ringing out, and Theo answers. "Donatello?"

"I need you to come home, T. You need to drop what you're doing and get back here now!"

"Why? What happened?"

"Where's Neo? Put him on the phone," Donatello orders.

"No, fucking tell me what the fuck is going on. *Or,* so help me God, I'll make sure you regret the day you invited me into your fucking home."

"It's Holly. She's okay. I got to the room before... I got there in time. But you need to get back here now."

"Holly?" Theo starts speaking in Italian. He's talking too fast, and I have no idea what he's saying. But I know he's scared. I can tell by the tone of his voice.

"T? I'm okay. I just need you to come and get me now, please." I try to maintain my composure.

"Dolcezza, talk to me. What happened? I'm on my way, okay? I'll be there real soon."

"Thank you," I say.

"Don't fucking hang up, Holly. What the fuck is going on?"

"I just need... I need you to..." What *do* I need? I don't even know. I need a shower. I need to wash the filth of that man from my body. And I need my husband.

"I'm going as fast as I can, dolcezza."

"I'll make sure the gates are open. We're in your room." Donatello hangs up, sliding the phone back into his pocket.

Then a thought occurs to me. I could be walking them right into a fucking trap. "Wait, how do I know you're not going to do something to T as soon as he steps through that door?" I ask Donatello, still aiming my gun at him.

"Because I give you my word. No harm will come to either of you in this house... again."

"Yeah, for some reason, your word isn't sitting too

well with me right now. I was meant to be safe here, and look what happened." I glance behind him, to where Sonnie's body lies still. I can't even begin to process that he's dead... that he *died* because of me.

"I know you have no reason to believe me, but I would never hurt you, Holly. I could never hurt *either* of you." There's nothing else for us to say or do, except wait for Theo to get here.

Chapter Twenty-Six

I jump out of the car before it even comes to a stop, running up the stairs and through the front doors with Neo right behind me calling out... *something*. I don't hear whatever it is. I have one thing on my mind: Holly. And God help anyone who gets in my way...

I race up to the second floor and draw my Glock from inside my jacket. And I'm glad I did as I round the corner and my eyes take in the scene in the hall. Three of my men are sprawled out, execution-style, their blood painting the white walls and splattering the ceiling. I'm stopped at the threshold by some wannabe thug. I don't think twice about pulling the trigger, putting a hole straight through the fucker's head.

The two men behind him point their weapons at me as I step forward. I make it to the first one, and by the time he hits the ground, the goon beside him is following suit—except it wasn't me who shot him. I spin around, my sight raised and ready, the exhilaration of the kill kicking in. Until my eyes land on hers...

Holly is standing with a gun raised in one hand, her other clutching at the fabric of her shirt. Her face is red, bruised. Someone fucking hit her, and everyone in this god-forsaken house is about to feel my wrath. I point the hot end of my barrel straight at Donatello. "What the fuck happened? Somebody better start fucking talking right the fuck now, before I empty this chamber in your fucking head."

"Theo, it wasn't his fault." Holly's voice is quiet as she falls to the floor.

"Fuck! Don't fucking move," I warn Donatello. Neo now has two guns trained on the old man. "Holly, dolcezza. What happened?" I remove my jacket and drape it over her shoulders, before picking her up and cradling her in my lap.

"He-he... I-I... I didn't know what to do, T. I'm

sorry. I killed him. I killed him," she says, her body shuddering. And it's not from the cold.

"Who?" I ask, looking up at Donatello. Holly is in no state to be talking right now.

"I heard the shots... By the time I got here, he was on fucking top of her... on the bed. I pulled him off, but she managed to pick up his gun. Shot him three times, perfect fucking aim." Donatello steps towards us, squatting down in front of Holly. "You did nothing wrong, bella. That cogliona was dead, whether you pulled the trigger or I did. You should feel nothing but pride, and anyone who says otherwise can come and see me."

"He was on..." I can't finish the sentence; my voice chokes up. I'm nauseous. I want to kill every mother-fucker in a five-mile radius.

"Theo, get her out of here. She needs you more than anything else right now. The rest can wait." Donatello breaks me from my rage-induced trance.

"How do I know you weren't a part of this?" I ask him. "That's your best fucking friend lying there, with half his skull missing and his brains pouring out. And you expect me to believe you're just okay with that?"

"Like I said, anyone who lays a hand on my family pays the goddamn price. I would have liked to make him suffer a bit more, but what's done is done." He walks straight past Neo and up to his men, all standing there with shock clear on their faces. "I want security increased. Spread the word: the Valentinos are fucking untouchable."

Holly's quiet sobs are killing me. I've showered her. I've held her. And I've tried to talk to her, but she won't say anything. It's breaking me to see her like this. To know that it's my fault for leaving her alone here. "Dolcezza, tell me what I can do? The doctor is waiting to see you, whenever you're ready. But we do need to get you looked at."

She shakes her head no, burying her face into my chest. Her arms are wrapped tightly around me. I rub my hands through her wet hair, and up and down her back. I'm out of my fucking element here. How the fuck do I fix this for her?

"Please, Holly, let the doctor check you over," I plead.

"Will you stay with me?" Her voice is hoarse, rough.

"I'm not going anywhere. I'll be right here, holding on to you the entire time," I promise her. I made sure Neo arranged for a female doctor, hoping that would ease her mind a little.

"Okay." Holly sits up, and her grip on me loosens a little, only to tighten again when I attempt to stand.

"I'm going to unlock the door. I'll be right back, dolcezza." Her eyes widen, and I know she doesn't want to let me go, but she does so reluctantly and just enough that I can slip out. I open the door and let the doctor in. "È traumatizzata e molto debole. Non toccarla da nessuna parte, senza prima chiederglielo. Se le fai del male, ti finisco, cazzo." I tell the doctor that Holly is traumatized and fragile, as well as give the woman a little friendly reminder that if she hurts my wife, I *will* kill her. "Come in. Holly, this is Dr. Lewis. She's going to ask you some questions and then conduct a quick examination, to make sure you're all right."

I'm not sure I can handle hearing Holly relay what happened; the version my imagination has cooked up is bad enough. I sit on the bed next to her, picking up her hand before offering it a reassuring squeeze. She slides in against me. If she were any closer, she'd be in my lap.

"Hello, Holly, it's lovely to meet you. My name is Allie Lewis. Do you mind if I take a quick look at the bump on your head?"

Holly turns to me, her eyes waiting for something, though I'm not sure what. I nod, urging her to continue. "Sure." Her voice is quiet as she gives her consent.

The doctor pokes around at the swelling that is currently covering the top half of Holly's face. "Are you nauseous? Did you black out at all when you were hit?"

"Ah, no. I was dizzy, but I didn't black out." My whole body tenses as she responds. The fact that she was hit *at all* makes me want to go off on a bloody rampage.

"Hm, it looks okay, but you need to be mindful of a concussion." The woman turns to me. "Wake her up every two hours. Throughout the night." I nod. *I can do that.* I'll do whatever I have to fucking do. "Holly, where else were you touched? Were you hit anywhere else?"

Holly stills, and silent tears roll down her cheeks. I swipe them away with my thumb. "It's okay, dolcezza. You need to tell the doctor. She needs to know, so she can do her job properly. He can't hurt you anymore. No one's gonna hurt you ever again," I whisper into her ear before kissing her forehead.

"He... he... um... My breasts, he grabbed my breasts," Holly admits.

"Okay, do you mind if I have a quick look?" The doctor's voice is soft and oddly soothing. I'm glad I had the forethought to request a female.

"Here, let me help." I peel Holly's robe open, but only enough to show the bruises that fucker left on her. I breathe in and count to ten in my head, conjuring up the various ways I want to bring the son of a bitch back to life, just so I can kill him again.

"Okay, these contusions should heal in a few days. Did he touch you anywhere else, dear? I know this may not be something you want to talk about or even recall.

But it's important we know everything that's happened to you. If you'd prefer some privacy, we can discuss it alone," the doctor offers.

"Like fuck you can! I'm not going anywhere. I'd like to see you fucking try to make me."

"With all due respect, Mr. Valentino, you are not my patient. Your wife is, and if she wants privacy, you will give it to her."

"No, I need Theo. He can't leave me," Holly rushes out, her fingernails digging into my palm as her grip on me tightens.

"Okay, if that's what you want, he can stay. I'm sorry, Holly. But I have to ask: did your attacker penetrate you?"

In other words: *was she fucking raped?* It's a question I haven't been able to ask her myself. Because I'm scared of hearing the fucking answer, equal parts needing to know and not wanting to believe it. I hold my breath and wait for Holly to respond. My thumb rubs little circles on her wrist.

"He... his fingers. It was his fingers."

Fuck! That fat fuck put his fucking fingers inside my wife. Inside *my* fucking wife. It's taking everything in me not to get up and let loose the monster clawing its way through my chest. I need to hurt someone—*a lot* of fucking someones. They need to pay for letting this happen. They all need to pay.

"Okay, do you want me to do a full examination? It's completely up to you, honey. You can say no."

"No." Holly is quick to answer.

"Okay." The woman pushes to her feet, before picking up her bag and tucking it under her arm. "Mr. Valentino, I'd like a word." Then she turns and walks out the door to wait for me in the hall.

"I'll be right back, dolcezza. I'm just going to stand in the doorway. I won't leave the room, I promise." I have to physically remove Holly's hand from mine, and I feel like a fucking asshole for doing so. I stop at the threshold, listening for the doctor to tell me whatever it is she wants to say.

"She's going to need help. This kind of trauma doesn't just go away. Make sure she has someone to talk to. A friend, a sister, a therapist. Anyone she can trust."

My first thought is Reilly. I should take Holly back to Sydney, so she can be with her sister. But selfishly, I want *that person* to be me. I want to be everything Holly needs. I don't bother responding to the woman. I simply nod my head and climb back into bed with my wife. She snuggles up against me, and I hold her tight.

It takes Holly an hour to fall asleep. I don't want to leave her. *I promised I wouldn't.* But I need fucking answers. I pull out my phone and text Neo, telling him to get me Donatello. I'm not prepared to leave my wife's side, so the son of a bitch can fucking meet me right outside this room. I untangle myself from Holly's grip and tiptoe towards the entryway, inching into the hall but leaving the door open a crack, so I can still see her.

Neo and Donatello are rounding the corner, both headed in my direction. He came alone. Without backup. He's either fucking stupid or brave. And right now, I'm not sure which. I tilt my head to the side, inspecting the old man's demeanor. I'm good at reading people. I always know when they're lying to me. "I have one question. Did you know that Giovani was planning to attack my wife?"

"No. If I knew, I would have slit his throat before he made it within two feet of that poor girl," he answers.

"You're oddly protective of my wife. Why?" I counter. I'm confused by his behavior. He's not lying. I can see the anger in his eyes at the mention of Holly's attack.

"She's family." He shrugs.

That's not the first time he's said that... "How so?"

Donatello sighs, running his hands through his hair. "You have to understand... I didn't know about this until that day you came to see me. I received a phone call during that meeting. Do you remember?" he asks. I nod my head. I recall him stepping out of the office. I overheard one side of a heated conversation.

When he returned, he stared at me for a long time, then he finally cleared his throat and we went back to talking business. "That call was from your mother. And that's the day I learned who you were, Theo. Had I known beforehand, I would have done something sooner. Brought you here earlier."

"What are you talking about?" He's making no fucking sense. *Who I am? Pretty sure I know who the fuck I am.*

"You're my son, Theo. That's why *your wife* is *my family*." His eyes are glassy, which says a lot for a made man. A Don. We learn at a very young age to mask any and all emotions.

"No, you're lying. My father is dead. And you aren't him," I growl.

"I'm sorry. I didn't know... I never would have let another man raise you."

"This can't be happening." I shake my head. No, this isn't true. I won't believe it. "Neo, have the jet ready to leave in thirty minutes." I walk back into the room and slam the door. Holly jumps at the sound. *Shit. Fuck.* I walk over and scoop her up into my arms.

"T, what's going on?" she asks groggily.

"We're going home," I whisper. "Go back to sleep. I'm taking you home, dolcezza."

Don't miss the final instalment of Theo and Holly's story in United Reign.

Made in the USA
Las Vegas, NV
17 July 2023